A BROKEN BETROTHAL

CONVENIENT ARRANGEMENTS (BOOK 1)

ROSE PEARSON

A BROKEN BETROTHAL

PROLOGUE

L ady Augusta looked at her reflection in the mirror and sighed inwardly. She had tried on almost every gown in her wardrobe and still was not at all decided on which one she ought to wear tonight. She had to make the right decision, given that this evening was to be her first outing into society since she had returned to London.

"Augusta, what in heaven's name...?" The sound of her mother's voice fading away as she looked all about the room and saw various gowns strewn everywhere, the maids quickening to stand straight, their heads bowed as the countess came into the room. Along with her came a friend of Lady Elmsworth, whom Augusta knew very well indeed, although it was rather embarrassing to have her step into the bedchamber when it was in such a disarray!

"Good afternoon, Mama," Augusta said, dropping into a quick curtsy. "And good afternoon, Lady Newfield." She took in Lady Newfield's face, seeing the twinkle in the lady's blue eyes and the way her lips twitched, which was in direct contrast to her mother, who was standing with her hands on her hips, clearly upset.

"Would you like to explain, my dear girl, what it is that you are doing here?" The countess looked into Augusta's face, her familiar dark eyes sharpening. Augusta tried to smile but her mother only narrowed her eyes and planted her hands on her hips, making it quite plain that she was greatly displeased with what Augusta was doing.

"Mama," Augusta wheedled, gesturing to her gowns. "You know that I must look my very best for this evening's ball. "Therefore, I must be certain that I—"

"We had already selected a gown, Augusta," Lady Elmsworth interrupted, quieting Augusta's excuses immediately. "You and I went to the dressmaker's only last week and purchased a few gowns that would be worn for this little Season. The first gown you were to wear was, if I recall, that primrose yellow." She indicated a gown that was draped over Augusta's bed, and Augusta felt heat rise into her face as the maids scurried to pick it up.

"I do not think it suits my coloring, Mama," she said, a little half-heartedly. "You are correct to state that we chose it together, but I have since reconsidered."

Lady Newfield cleared her throat, with Lady Elmsworth darting a quick look towards her.

"I would be inclined to agree, Lady Elmsworth," she said, only for Lady Elmsworth to throw up one hand, bringing her friend's words to a swift end. Augusta's hopes died away as her mother's thin brows began knitting together with displeasure. "That is enough, Augusta," she said firmly, ignoring Lady Newfield entirely. "That gown will do you very well, just as we discussed." She looked at the maids. "Tidy the rest of these up at once and ensure that the primrose yellow is left for this evening."

The maids curtsied and immediately set to their task, leaving Augusta to merely sit and watch as the maids obeyed the mistress of the house rather than doing what she wanted. In truth, the gown that had been chosen for her had been mostly her mother's choice, whilst she had attempted to make gentle protests that had mostly been ignored. With her dark brown hair and green eyes, Augusta was sure that the gown did, in fact, suit her coloring very well, but she did not want to be clad in yellow, not when so many other debutantes would be wearing the same. No, Augusta wanted to stand out, to be set apart, to be noticed! She had come to London only a few months ago for the Season and had been delighted when her father had encouraged them to return for the little Season. Thus, she had every expectation of finding a suitable husband and making a good match. However, given how particular her mother was being over her gown, Augusta began to worry that her mother would soon begin to choose Augusta's dance partners and the like so that she would have no independence whatsoever!

"I think I shall return to our tea," Lady Newfield said gently as Lady Elmsworth gave her friend a jerky nod. "I apologize for the intrusion, Lady Augusta."

"There was no intrusion," Augusta said quickly, seeing the small smile that ran around Lady Newfield's mouth and wishing that her mother had been a little more willing to listen to her friend's comments. For whatever reason, she felt as though Lady Newfield understood her reasoning more than her mother did.

"Now, Augusta," Lady Elmsworth said firmly, settling herself in a chair near to the hearth where a fire burned brightly, chasing away the chill of a damp winter afternoon. "This evening, you are to be introduced to one gentleman in particular. I want you to ensure that you behave impeccably. Greet him warmly and correctly, but thereafter, do not say a good deal."

Augusta frowned, her eyes searching her mother's face for answers that Lady Elmsworth was clearly unwilling to give. "Might I ask why I am to do such a thing, Mama?"

Lady Elmsworth held Augusta's gaze for a moment, and then let out a small sigh. "You will be displeased, of course, for you are always an ungrateful sort but nonetheless, you ought to find some contentment in this." She waited a moment as though waiting to see if Augusta had some retort prepared already, only to shrug and then continue. "Your father has found you a suitable match, Augusta. You are to meet him this evening."

The world seemed to stop completely as Augusta stared at her mother in horror. The footsteps of the maids came to silence; the quiet crackling of the fire turned to naught. Her chest heaved with great breaths as Augusta tried to accept what she had just been told, closing her eyes to shut out the view of her mother's slightly bored expression. This was not what she had expected. Coming back to London had been a matter of great excitement for her, having been told that *this* year would be the year for her to make a suitable match. She had never once thought that such a thing would be pulled from her, removed from her grasp entirely. Her father had never once mentioned that he would be doing such a thing but now, it seemed, he had chosen to do so without saying a word to her about his intentions.

"Do try to form some response, Augusta," Lady Elmsworth said tiredly. "I am aware this is something of a surprise, but it is for your own good. The gentleman in question has an excellent title and is quite wealthy." She waved a hand in front of her face as though such things were the only things in the world that mattered. "It is not as though you could have found someone on your own, Augusta."

"I should have liked the opportunity to try," Augusta whispered, hardly able to form the words she wanted so desperately to say.

"You had the summer Season," Lady Elmsworth retorted with a shrug. "Do you not recall?"

Augusta closed her eyes. The summer Season had been her first outing into society, and she had enjoyed every moment of it. Her father and mother had made it quite plain that this was not to be the year where she found a husband but rather a time for her to enjoy society, to become used to what it meant to live as a member of the *ton*. The little Season and the summer Season thereafter, she had been told, would be the ones for her to seek out a husband.

And now, that had been pulled away from her before she had even had the opportunity to be amongst the gentlemen of the *beau monde*.

"As I have said," Lady Elmsworth continued, briskly, ignoring Augusta's complaint and the clear expression of shock on her face, "there is no need for you to do anything other than dress in the gown we chose together and then to ensure that you greet Lord Pendleton with all refinement and propriety."

Augusta closed her eyes. "Lord Pendleton?" she repeated, tremulously, already afraid that this gentleman was some older, wealthy gentleman who, for whatever reason, had not been able to find a wife and thus had been more than eager to accept her father's offer.

"Did I not say?" Lady Elmsworth replied, sounding somewhat distracted. She rose quickly, her skirts swishing noisily as she walked towards the door. "He is brother to the Marquess of Leicestershire. A fine gentleman, by all accounts." She shrugged. "He is quiet and perhaps a little dull, but he will do very well for you." One of the maids held the door open, and before Augusta could say more, her mother swept out of the room and the door was closed tightly behind her.

Augusta waited for tears to come but they did not even begin to make their way towards her eyes. She was numb all over, cold and afraid of what was to come. This was not something she had even considered a possibility when it came to her own considerations for what the little Season would hold. There had always been the belief that she would be able to dance, converse, and laugh with as many gentlemen as thought to seek her out. In time, there would be courtships and one gentleman in particular might bring themselves to her notice. There would be excitement and anticipation, nights spent reading and re-reading notes and letters from the gentleman in question, her heart quickening at the thought of marrying him.

But now, such thoughts were gone from her. There was to be none of what she had expected, what she had hoped for. Instead, there was to be a meeting and an arrangement, with no passion or excitement.

Augusta closed her eyes and finally felt a sting of tears. Dropping her head into her hands, she let her emotions roar to life, sending waves of feeling crashing through her until, finally, Augusta wept.

CHAPTER ONE

Quite why he had arranged to be present this evening, Stephen did not know. He ought to have stated that he would meet Lady Augusta in a quieter setting than a ball so that he might have talked with her at length rather than forcing a quick meeting upon them both in a room where it was difficult to hear one's own voice such was the hubbub of the crowd.

He sighed and looked all about him again, finding no delight in being in the midst of society once more. He was a somewhat retiring gentleman, finding no pleasure in the gossip and rumors that flung themselves all around London during the little Season, although it was always much worse during the summer Season. Nor did he appreciate the falseness of those who came to speak and converse with him, knowing full well that the only reason they did so was to enquire after his brother, the Marquess of Leicestershire.

His brother was quite the opposite in both looks and

character, for where Stephen had light brown hair with blue eyes, his brother had almost black hair with dark brown eyes that seemed to pierce into the very soul of whomever he was speaking with. The ladies of the *ton* wanted nothing more than to be in the presence of Lord Leicestershire and, given he was absent from society, they therefore came towards Stephen in order to find out what they could about his brother.

It was all quite wearisome, and Stephen did not enjoy even a moment of it. He was not as important as his brother, he knew, given he did not hold the high title nor have the same amount of wealth as Lord Leicestershire, but surely his own self, his conversation and the like, was of *some* interest? He grinned wryly to himself as he picked up a glass from the tray held by a footman, wondering silently to himself that, if he began to behave as his brother had done on so many occasions, whether or not that would garner him a little more interest from rest of the *ton*.

"You look much too contented," said a familiar voice, and Stephen looked to his left to see his acquaintance, Lord Dryden, approach him. Lord Dryden, a viscount, had an estate near the border to Scotland and, whilst lower in title than Stephen, had become something of a close acquaintance these last two years.

"Lord Dryden," Stephen grinned, slapping the gentleman on the back. "How very good to see you again."

Lord Dryden chuckled. "And you," he said with an honest look in his eyes. "Now, tell me why you are standing here smiling to yourself when I know very well that a ball is not the sort of event you wish to attend?"

Stephen's grin remained on his lips, his eyes alighting on various young ladies that swirled around him. "I was merely considering what my life might be like if I chose to live as my brother does," he answered, with a shrug. "I should have all of society chasing after me, I suppose, although a good many would turn their heads away from me with the shame of being in my company."

"That is quite true," Lord Dryden agreed, no smile on his face but rather a look of concern. "You do not wish to behave so, I hope?"

"No, indeed, I do not," Stephen answered firmly, his smile fading away. "I confess that I am growing weary of so many in the *ton* coming to seek me out simply because they wish to know more about my brother."

"He is not present this evening?"

Stephen snorted. "He is not present for the little Season," he replied with a shrug of his shoulders. "Do not ask me what he has been doing, or why he has such a notable absence, for I fear I cannot tell you." Setting his shoulders, he let out a long breath. "No, I must look to my future."

"Indeed," Lord Dryden responded, an interested look on his face as he eyed Stephen speculatively. "And what is it about your future that you now consider?"

Stephen cleared his throat, wondering whether he ought to tell his friend even though such an arrangement had not yet been completely finalized. "I am to consider myself betrothed very soon," he said before he lost his nerve and kept such news to himself. "I am to meet the lady here this evening. Her father has already signed the papers and they await me in my study." He shrugged one shoulder. "I am sure that, provided she has not lost all of her teeth and that her voice is pleasant enough, the betrothal will go ahead as intended."

Lord Dryden stared at Stephen for a few moments, visible shock rippling over his features. His eyes were wide and his jaw slack, without even a single flicker of mirth in his gaze as he looked back at him. Stephen felt his stomach drop, now worried that Lord Dryden would make some remark that would then force Stephen to reconsider all that he had decided thus far, fearful now that he had made some foolish mistake.

"Good gracious!" Lord Dryden began to laugh, his hand grasping Stephen's shoulder tightly. "You are betrothed?" Shaking his head, he let out another wheezing laugh before straightening and looking Stephen directly in the eye. "I should have expected such a thing from you, I suppose, given you are always entirely practical and very well-considered, but I had not expected it so soon!"

"So soon?" Stephen retorted with a chuckle. "I have been in London for the last three Seasons and have found not even a single young lady to be interested in even conversing with me without needing to talk solely about my brother." His lip curled, a heaviness sitting back on his shoulders as he let out a long sigh. "Therefore, this seemed to be the wisest and the most practical of agreements."

Lord Dryden chuckled again, his eyes still filled with good humor. "I am glad to hear it," he said warmly. "I do congratulate you, of course! Pray, forgive me for my humor. It is only that it has come as something of a surprise to hear such a thing from you yet, now that I consider it, it makes a good deal of sense!" He chuckled again and the sound began to grate on Stephen, making him frown as he returned his friend's sharp look.

Lord Dryden did not appear to care, even if he did notice Stephen's ire. Instead, he leaned a little closer, his eyes bright with curiosity. "Pray, tell me," he began as Stephen nodded, resigning himself to a good many questions. "Who is this lady? Is she of good quality?"

"Very good, yes," Stephen replied, aware, while he did not know the lady's features or character, that she came from a good family line and that breeding would not be a cause for concern. "She is Lady Augusta, daughter to the Earl of Elmsworth."

Lord Dryden's eyes widened, and his smile faded for a moment. "Goodness," he said quietly, looking at Stephen as though he feared his friend had made some sort of dreadful mistake. "And you have met the lady in question?"

"I am to meet her this evening," Stephen answered quickly, wondering why Lord Dryden now appeared so surprised. "I have not heard anything disreputable about her, however." He narrowed his gaze and looked at his friend sharply. "Why? Have you heard some rumor I have not?"

Lord Dryden held up both his hands in a gesture of defense. "No, indeed not!" he exclaimed, sounding quite horrified. "No, tis only that she is a lady who is very well thought of in society. She is well known to everyone, seeks to converse with them all, and has a good many admirers." One shoulder lifted in a half shrug. "To know that her father has sought out an arrangement for her surprises me a little, that is all."

"Because she could do very well without requiring an arrangement," Stephen said slowly understanding what Lord Dryden meant. "Her father appeared to be quite eager to arrange such a thing, however." He sighed and looked all about him, wondering when Lord Elmsworth and his daughter would appear. "He and I spoke at Whites when the matter of his daughter came up."

"And the arrangement came from there?" Lord Dryden asked as Stephen nodded. "I see." He lapsed into silence for a moment, then nodded as though satisfied that he had asked all the questions he wished. "Very good. Then may I be the first to congratulate you!" Lord Dryden's smile returned, and he held out a hand for Stephen to shake. Stephen did so after only a momentary hesitation, reminding himself that there was not, as yet, a complete agreement between himself and Lord Elmsworth.

"I still have to sign and return the papers," he reminded Lord Dryden, who made a noise in the back of his throat before shrugging. "You do not think there will be any difficulty there, I presume?"

"Of course there will not be any difficulty," Lord Dryden retorted with a roll of his eyes. "Lady Augusta is very pleasing, indeed. I am sure you will have no partic-ular difficulty with her."

Stephen opened his mouth to respond, only to see someone begin to approach him. His heart quickened in his chest as he looked at them a little more carefully, seeing Lord Elmsworth approaching and, with him, a young lady wearing a primrose yellow gown. She had an elegant and slender figure and was walking in a most demure fashion, with eyes that lingered somewhere near his knees rather than looking up into people's faces. Her dark brown hair was pulled away from her face, with one or two small ringlets tumbling down near her temples, so as to soften the severity of it. When she dared a glance at him, he was certain he caught a hint of emerald green in her eyes. Almost immediately, her gaze returned to the floor as she dropped into a curtsy, Lord Elmsworth only a step or two in front of her.

"Lord Pendleton!" Lord Elmsworth exclaimed, shaking Stephen's hand with great enthusiasm. "Might I present my daughter, Lady Augusta." He beamed at his daughter, who was only just rising from what had been a perfect curtsy.

"Good evening, Lady Augusta," Stephen said, bowing before her. "I presume your father has already made quite plain who I am?" He looked keenly into her face, and when she lifted her eyes to his, he felt something strike at his heart.

It was not warmth, however, nor a joy that she was quietly beautiful. It did not chime with happiness or contentment but rather with a warning. A warning that Lady Augusta was not as pleased with this arrangement as he. A warning that he might come to trouble if he continued as had been decided. She was looking at him with a hardness in her gaze that hit him hard. There was a coldness, a reserve in her expression, that he could not escape. Clearly, Lady Augusta was not at all contented with the arrangement her father had made for her, which, in turn, did not bode well for him.

"Yes," Lady Augusta said after a moment or two, her voice just as icy as her expression. "Yes, my father has informed of who you are, Lord Pendleton." She looked away, her chin lifted, clearly finding there to be no desire otherwise to say anything more.

Stephen cleared his throat, glancing towards Lord Dryden, who was, to his surprise, not watching Lady Augusta as he had expected, but rather had his attention focused solely on Lord Elmsworth. There was a dark frown on his face; his eyes narrowed just a little and a clear dislike began to ripple across his expression. What was it that Lord Dryden could see that Stephen himself could not?

"Might I introduce Viscount Dryden?" he said quickly, before he could fail in his duties. "Viscount Dryden, this is the Earl of Elmsworth and his daughter—"

"We are already acquainted," Lord Dryden interrupted, bowing low before lifting his head, looking nowhere but at Lady Augusta. "It is very pleasant to see you again, Lady Augusta. I hope you are enjoying the start of the little Season."

Something in her expression softened, and Stephen saw Lady Augusta's mouth curve into a gentle smile. She answered Lord Dryden politely and Stephen soon found himself growing a little embarrassed at the easy flow of conversation between his friend and his betrothed. There was not that ease of manner within himself, he realized, dropping his head just a little so as to regain his sense of composure.

"Perhaps I might excuse myself for a short time," Lord Elmsworth interrupted before Lord Dryden could ask Lady Augusta another question. "Lady Elmsworth is standing but a short distance away and will be watching my daughter closely."

Stephen glanced to his right and saw an older lady looking directly at him, her sense of haughtiness rushing towards him like a gust of wind. There was no contentment in her eyes, but equally, there was no dislike either. Rather, there was the simple expectation that this was how things were to be done and that they ought to continue without delay.

"But of course, Lord Elmsworth," Stephen said quickly, bowing slightly. "I should like to sign your daughter's dance card, if I may?"

"I think," came Lady Augusta's voice, sharp and brittle, "then if that is the case, you ought to be asking the lady herself whether or not she has any space remaining on her card for you to do such a thing, Lord Pendleton."

There came an immediate flush of embarrassment onto Stephen's face, and he cleared his throat whilst Lord Elmsworth sent a hard glance towards his daughter, which she ignored completely. Only Lord Dryden chuckled, the sound breaking the tension and shattering it into a thousand pieces as Stephen looked away.

"You are quite correct to state such a thing, Lady Augusta," Lord Dryden said, easily. "You must forgive my friend. I believe he was a little apprehensive about this meeting and perhaps has forgotten quite how things are done."

Stephen's smile was taut, but he forced it to his lips regardless. "But of course, Lady Augusta," he said tightly. "Might you inform me whether or not you have any spaces on your dance card that I might then be able to take from you?" He bowed his head and waited for her to respond, seeing Lord Elmsworth move away from them all without waiting to see what his daughter would say.

"I thank you for your kind consideration in requesting such a thing from me," Lady Augusta answered, a little too saucily for his liking. "Yes, I believe I do have a few spaces, Lord Pendleton. Please, choose whichever you like." She handed him her dance card and then pulled her hand back, the ribbon sliding from her wrist as he looked down at it. She turned her head away as if she did not want to see where he wrote his name, and this, in itself, sent a flurry of anger down Stephen's spine. What was wrong with this young lady? Was she not glad that she was now betrothed, that she would soon have a husband and become mistress of his estate?

For a moment, he wondered if he had made a mistake in agreeing to this betrothal, feeling a swell of relief in his chest that he had not yet signed the agreement, only for Lord Dryden to give him a tiny nudge, making him realize he had not yet written his name down on the dance card but was, in fact, simply staring at it as though it might provide him with all the answers he required.

"The country dance, mayhap," he said, a little more loudly than he had intended. "Would that satisfy you, Lady Augusta?"

She turned her head and gave him a cool look, no smile gracing her lips. "But of course," she said with more sweetness than he had expected. "I would be glad to dance with you, Lord Pendleton. The country dance sounds quite wonderful."

He frowned, holding her gaze for a moment longer before dropping his eyes back to her dance card again and writing his name there. Handing it back to her, he waited for her to smile, to acknowledge what he had given her, only for her to sniff, bob a curtsy and turn away. Stephen's jaw worked furiously, but he remained standing steadfastly watching after her, refusing to allow himself to chase after her and demand to know what she meant by such behavior. Instead, he kept his head lifted and his eyes fixed, thinking to himself that he had, most likely, made a mistake.

"I would ascertain from her behavior that this betrothal has come as something of a shock," Lord Dryden murmured, coming closer to Stephen and looking after Lady Augusta with interest. "She was less than pleased to be introduced to you, that is for certain!"

Stephen blew out his frustration in a long breath, turning his eyes away from Lady Augusta and looking at his friend. "I think I have made a mistake," he said gruffly. "That young lady will not do at all! She is—"

"She is overcome," Lord Dryden interrupted, holding up one hand to stem the protest from Stephen's lips. "As I have said, I think this has been something of a shock to her. You may recall that I said I am acquainted with Lady Augusta already and I know that how she presented herself this evening is not her usual character."

Stephen shook his head, his lips twisting as he considered what he was to do. "I am not certain that I have made the wisest decision," he said softly. "Obviously, I require a wife and that does mean that I shall have to select someone from amongst the *ton*, but—"

"Lady Augusta is quite suitable," Lord Dryden interrupted firmly. "And, if you were quite honest with yourself, Lord Pendleton, I think you would find that such an arrangement suits you very well. After all—" He gestured to the other guests around him. "You are not at all inclined to go out amongst the *ton* and find a lady of your choosing, are you?"

Stephen sighed heavily and shot Lord Dryden a wry look. "That is true enough, I suppose."

"Then trust me when I say that Lady Augusta is more than suitable for you," Lord Dryden said again, with such fervor that Stephen felt as though he had no other choice to believe him. "Sign the betrothal agreement and know that Lady Augusta will not be as cold towards you in your marriage as she has been this evening." He chuckled and slapped Stephen on the shoulder. "May I be the first to offer you my congratulations."

Smiling a little wryly, Stephen found himself nodding. "Very well," he told Lord Dryden. "I accept your congratulations with every intention of signing the betrothal agreement when I return home this evening."

"Capital!" Lord Dryden boomed, looking quite satisfied with himself. "Then I look forward to attending your wedding in the knowledge that it was I who brought it about." He chuckled and then, spotting a young lady coming towards him quickly excused himself. Stephen smiled as he saw Lord Dryden offer his arm to the young lady and then step out on to the floor. His friend was correct. Lady Augusta was, perhaps, a little overwhelmed with all that had occurred and simply was not yet open to the fact that she would soon be his wife. In time, she would come to be quite happy with him and their life together; he was sure of it. He had to thrust his worries aside and accept his decisions for what they were.

"I shall sign it the moment I return home," he said aloud to himself as though confirming this was precisely what he intended to do. With a small sigh of relief at his decision, he lifted his chin and set his shoulders. Within the week, everyone would know of his betrothal to Lady Augusta and that, he decided, brought him a good deal of satisfaction.

HIS QUILL HOVERED over the line for just a moment but, with a clenching of his jaw, Stephen signed his name on the agreement. His breath shot out of him with great fury, leaving him swallowing hard, realizing what he had done. It was now finalized. He would marry Lady Augusta, and the banns would have to be called very soon, given her father wanted her wed before the end of the little Season. Letting out his breath slowly, he rolled up the papers and began to prepare his seal, only for there to come a hurried knock at the door. He did not even manage to call out for his servant to enter, for the butler rushed in before he could open his mouth.

"Do forgive me, my lord," the butler exclaimed, breathing hard from his clear eagerness to reach Stephen in time. "This came from your brother's estate with a most urgent request that you read it at once."

Startled, his stomach twisting one way and then the other, Stephen took the note from the butler's hand and opened it, noting that there was no print on the seal. His heart began to pound as he read the news held within.

"My brother is dead," he whispered, one hand gripping onto the edge of his desk for support. "He...he was shot in a duel and died on the field." Closing his eyes, Stephen let the news wash over him, feeling all manner of strong emotions as he fought to understand what had occurred. His brother had passed away, then, lost to the grave, and out of nothing more than his foolishness. To have been fighting in a duel meant that Leicestershire had done something of the most grievous nature—whether it had been stealing another man's wife or taking affections from some unfortunate young lady without any intention of pursuing the matter further.

Running one hand over his face, Stephen felt the weight of his grief come to settle on his heart, his whole body seeming to ache with a pain he had only experienced once before when their dear father had passed away. His throat constricted as he thought of his mother. He would have to go to her at once, to comfort her in the midst of her sorrow. Yes, his brother had packed her off to the Dower House long before she was due to reside there, and yes, there had been some difficulties between them, but Stephen knew that she had loved her eldest son and would mourn the loss of him greatly.

A groan came from his lips as he lifted his head and tried to focus on his butler. His vision was blurry, his head feeling heavy and painful.

"Ready my carriage at once," he rasped, "and have my things sent after me. I must return to my brother's estate."

The butler bowed. "At once," he said, his concern clear in his wide-eyed expression. "I beg your pardon for my intrusion, my lord, but is Lord Leicestershire quite well?"

Stephen looked at his faithful butler, knowing that the man had worked for the family for many years in keeping the townhouse in London readied for them and understood that his concern was genuine. "My brother is dead," he said hoarsely as the butler gasped in horror. "I have lost him. He is gone, and I shall never see him again."

CHAPTER TWO

S ix months later

AUGUSTA ROLLED her eyes as her mother brought out
the primrose yellow dress that she had worn at the start of
the little Season some six months ago. She sighed as her
mother spread it out with one hand, a look in her eye that
told Augusta she was not about to escape this easily.

"That gown was for the winter, Mama," she said,
calmly. "I cannot wear it again now that the sun is
shining and the air is so very warm." She gestured to it
with a look of what she hoped was sadness on her face.
"Besides, it is not quite up to the fashion for this current
Season."

Her mother tutted. "Nonsense, Augusta," she said
briskly. "There is very little need for you to purchase new
gowns when you are to have a trousseau. Your betrothed

has, as you know, recently lost his brother and as such, will need to find some happiness in all that he does. I must hope that your presence will bring him a little joy in his sorrow and, in wearing the very same gown as you were first introduced to him in, I am certain that Lord Pendleton—I mean, Lord Leicestershire—will be very happy to see you again."

Augusta said nothing, silently disagreeing with her mother and having no desire whatsoever to greet her betrothed again, whether in her primrose yellow gown or another gown entirely. She had felt compassion and sympathy for his loss, yes, but she had silently reveled in her newfound freedom. Indeed, given their betrothal had not yet been confirmed and given the *ton* knew nothing of it, Augusta had spent the rest of the little Season enjoying herself, silently ignoring the knowledge that within the next few months, she would have to let everyone in the *ton* know of her engagement.

But not yet, it seemed. She had spoken to her father, and he had confirmed that the papers had not been returned by Lord Leicestershire but had urged her not to lose hope, stating that he had every reason to expect the gentleman to do just as he had promised but that he was permitting him to have some time to work through his grief before pressing him about the arrangement.

And when news had been brought that the new Marquess of Leicestershire had come to London for the Season, her father had taken it as confirmation that all was just as it ought to be. He was quite contented with the situation as things stood, silently certain that when

Lord Leicestershire was ready, he would approach the Earl himself or speak directly to Augusta.

"I will not wear that gown, Mama," Augusta said frostily. "I am well aware of what you hope for but I cannot agree. That gown is not at all suitable for Lord Stonington's ball! I must find something that is quite beautiful, Mama." She saw her mother frown and tried quickly to come up with some reason for her to agree to such a change. "I know your intentions are good," she continued, swiftly, "but Lord Leicestershire will be glad to see me again no matter what I am wearing; I am sure of it. And, Mama, if I wear the primrose yellow gown, might it not remind him of the night that he was told of his brother's death?" She let her voice drop low, her eyes lowering dramatically. "The night when he had no other choice but to run from London so that he might comfort his mother and tidy up the ruin his brother left behind."

"Augusta!" Lady Elmsworth's voice was sharp. "Do not speak in such a callous manner!"

Augusta, who was nothing if not practical, looked at her mother askance. "I do not consider speaking the truth plainly to be callous, Mama," she said quite calmly. "After all, it is not as though Lord Leicestershire's brother was anything other than a scoundrel." She shrugged, turning away from her mother and ignoring the horrified look on her face. "Everyone in London is well aware what occurred."

She herself had been unable to escape the gossip and, to her shame, had listened to it eagerly at times. The late Lord Leicestershire had lost his life in a duel that had not gone well for him. He had taken a young lady of quality and attempted to steal kisses—and perhaps more—from her, only to be discovered by the young lady's brother, who was a viscount of some description. Despite the fact that such duels were frowned upon, one had taken place and the gentleman who had done such a dreadful thing to a young lady of society had paid the ultimate price for his actions. A part of her did feel very sorry indeed for the newly titled Lord Leicestershire, knowing that he must have had to endure a good deal of struggle, difficulty and pain in realizing not only what his brother had done but in taking on all the responsibilities that now came with his new title.

"I should think you better than to listen to gossip," Lady Elmsworth said, primly. "Now, Augusta, do stop being difficult and wear what I ask of you."

"No," Augusta replied quite firmly, surprising both herself and her mother with her vehemence. "No, I shall not." Taking in the look of astonishment on her mother's face, Augusta felt her spirits lift very high indeed as she realized that, if she spoke with determination, her mother might, in fact, allow her to do as she wished. She had, thus far, always bowed to her mother's authority, but ever since she had discovered that her marriage was already planned for her and that she was to have no independence whatsoever, she had found a small spark growing steadily within her. A spark that determined that she find some way to have a little autonomy, even if it would only be for a short time.

"I will wear the light green silk," she said decisively,

walking to her wardrobe and indicating which one she meant. "It brings out my complexion a little more, I think." She smiled to herself and touched the fabric gently. "And I believe it brings a little more attention to my eyes."

Lady Elmsworth sighed heavily but, thankfully, she set down the primrose yellow and then proceeded to seat herself in a chair by the fire, which was not lit today given the warmth of the afternoon. "You think this is the most suitable choice, then?"

"I do," Augusta said firmly. "I shall wear this and have a few pearls and perhaps a ribbon set into my hair." Again, she smiled but did not see her mother's dark frown. "And perhaps that beautiful diamond pendant around my neck."

Lady Elmsworth's frown deepened. "You need not try to draw attention to yourself, Augusta," she reminded her sternly. "You are betrothed. You will be wed to Lord Leicestershire and he is the only one you need attempt to impress."

Augusta hid the sigh from her mother as she turned back to her wardrobe, closing the door carefully so as not to crush any of her gowns. A part of her hoped that she would not have to marry Lord Leicestershire, for given he had not yet returned the betrothal agreement to her father, there seemed to be no eagerness on his part to do so or to proceed with their engagement. Mayhap, now that he was of a great and high title, he might find himself a little more interested in the young ladies of the *ton* and would not feel the need to sign the betrothal agreement at all. It might all come to a very satisfactory close, and she could have the freedom she had always expected.

"Augusta!" Lady Elmsworth's voice was sharp, as though she knew precisely what it was Augusta was thinking. "You will make sure that all of your attention is on your betrothed this evening. Do you understand me?"

"We are not betrothed yet, Mama," Augusta replied a little tartly. "Therefore, I cannot show him any specific attention for fear of what others might say." She arched one eyebrow and looked at her mother as she turned around, aware she was irritating her parent but finding a dull sense of satisfaction in her chest. "Once the agreement has been sent to Papa, then, of course, I shall do my duty." She dropped into a quick curtsy, her eyes low and her expression demure, but it did not fool Lady Elmsworth.

"You had best be very careful with your behavior this evening, Augusta," she exclaimed, practically throwing herself from her chair as she rose to her feet, her cheeks a little pink and her eyes blazing with an unexpressed frustration. "I shall be watching you most carefully."

"Of course, Mama," Augusta replied quietly, permitting herself a small smile as her mother left the room, clearly more than a little irritated with all that Augusta had said. Augusta let a long breath escape her, feeling a sense of anticipation and anxiety swirl all about within her as she considered what was to come this evening. Lord Leicestershire would be present, she knew, for whilst he had not written to her directly to say such a thing, all of London was abuzz with the news that the new Marquess had sent his acceptance to

Lord Stonington's ball. Everyone would want to look at him, to see his face and to wonder just how like his brother he might prove to be. Everyone, of course, except for Augusta. She would greet him politely, of course, but had no intention of showing any interest in him whatsoever. Perhaps that, combined with his new title and his new appreciation from the *ton,* might decide that she was no longer a suitable choice for a wife.

Augusta could only hope.

"GOOD EVENING, LADY AUGUSTA."

Augusta gasped in surprise as she turned to see who had spoken her name, before throwing herself into the arms of a lovely lady. "Lady Mary!" she cried, delighted to see her dear friend again. They had shared one Season already as debutantes and had become very dear friends indeed, and Augusta had missed her at the little Season. "How very glad I am to see you again. I am in desperate need of company and you have presented yourself to me at the very moment that I need you!"

Lady Mary laughed and squeezed Augusta's hand. "But of course," she said, a twinkle in her eye. "I knew very well that you would need a dear friend to walk through this Season with you—just as I need one also!" She turned and looked at the room, the swirling colors of the gowns moving all around them, and let out a contented sigh. "I am quite certain that this Season, we shall both find a suitable match, and I, for one, am eagerly looking forward to the courtship, the excitement and the wonderfulness that is sure to follow!"

Augusta could not join in with the delight that Lady Mary expressed, her heart suddenly heavy and weighted as it dropped in her chest. Lady Mary noticed at once, her joyous smile fading as she looked into Augusta's face.

"My dear friend, whatever is the matter?"

Augusta opened her mouth to answer, only for her gaze to snag on something. Or, rather, a familiar face that seemed to loom out of the crowd towards her, her heart slamming hard as she realized who it was.

"Lady Augusta?"

Lady Mary's voice seemed to be coming from very far away as Augusta's eyes fixed upon Lord Leicestershire, her throat constricting and a sudden pain stabbing into her chest. He was standing a short distance away, and even though there were other guests coming in and out of her vision, blocking her view of him entirely upon occasion, she seemed to be able to see him quite clearly. His eyes were fixed to hers, appearing narrowed and dark and filled with nothing akin to either gladness or relief upon seeing her. Her stomach dropped to the floor for an inexplicable reason, making her wonder if he felt the same about her as she did about him. Why did that trouble her, she wondered, unable to tug her gaze from his. She should be able to turn her head away from him at once, should be able to show the same disregard as she had done at their first meeting, should be able to express her same dislike for their arrangement as she had done at the first—but for whatever reason, she was not able to do it.

"Lady Augusta, you are troubling me now!"

Lady Mary's voice slowly came back to her ears, growing steadily louder until the hubbub of the room appeared to be much louder than before. She closed her eyes tightly, finally freed from Lord Leicestershire's gaze, and felt her whole body tremble with a strange shudder.

"Lady Mary," she breathed, her hand touching her friend's arm. "I—I apologize. It is only that I have seen my betrothed and I—"

"Your betrothed?"

Lady Mary's eyes widened, her cheeks rapidly losing their color as she stared at Augusta with evident concern.

"You are engaged?" Lady Mary whispered as Augusta's throat tightened all the more. "When did such a thing occur?"

Augusta shook her head minutely. "It was not something of my choosing," she answered hoarsely. "My father arranged it on my behalf, without my knowledge of it. When I was present in the little Season, I was introduced to Lord Pendleton."

"Lord Pendleton?" Lady Mary exclaimed, only to close her eyes in embarrassment and drop her head.

Augusta smiled tightly. "Indeed," she said, seeing her friend's reaction and fully expecting her to be aware of the situation regarding Lord Pendleton. "He has not signed the betrothal agreement as far as I am aware, for it has not yet been returned to my father. However, given he has been in mourning for his brother, my father has not been overly eager in pursuing the matter, believing that Lord Leicestershire—as he is now—will return the papers when he is quite ready."

Lady Mary said nothing for some moments, considering all that had been said carefully and letting her eyes rove towards where Augusta had been looking towards only a few moments before.

"That is most extraordinary," she said, one hand now pressed against her heart. "And might I inquire as to whether or not you are pleased with this arrangement?"

With a wry smile, Augusta said nothing but looked at her friend with a slight lift of her eyebrow, making Lady Mary more than aware of precisely how she felt.

"I see," Lady Mary replied, her eyes still wide but seeming to fill with sympathy as she squeezed Augusta's hand, her lips thin. "I am sorry that you have had to endure such difficulties. I cannot imagine what you must have felt to be told that your marriage was all arranged without you having any awareness of such a thing beforehand!"

"It has been rather trying," Augusta admitted softly. "I have a slight hope through it all, however."

"Oh?"

Allowing herself another smile, Augusta dared a glance back towards Lord Leicestershire, only to see him still watching her. Embarrassed, she pulled her eyes away quickly, looking back to her friend. "I have a slight hope that he might decide *not* to sign the papers," she said as Lady Mary sucked in a breath. "As he is now a marquess and an heir, what if he decides that he must now choose his bride with a good deal more consideration?" Feeling a little more relaxed, no longer as anxious and as confused as she had been only a few moments before, she allowed herself a small smile. "I might be able to discover my freedom once more."

Lady Mary did not smile. Rather, her lips twisted to one side, and her brows lowered. "But would that not then mean that your father might, once again, find you another match of his choosing?" she said quietly, as though she were afraid to upset Augusta any further. "Lord Leicestershire is certainly an excellent match, Lady Augusta. He is a marquess and will have an excellent fortune. Surely he is not to be dismissed with such ease!"

Augusta allowed herself to frown, having not considered such a thing before. She did not want to be saddled with anyone of her father's choosing, instead wanting to discover a husband of her own choice. There was that choice there that, up until the previous little Season, she had always expected to have.

"I will simply speak to my father," she said airily, trying to express some sort of expectation that her father would do precisely what she asked. "He will be willing to listen to me, I am sure."

Lady Mary's expression cleared. "Well, if that is true, then I must hope that you can extricate yourself from this...if you so wish." That flickering frown remained, reminding Augusta that she was now betrothed to a marquess. A Marquess who had influence, wealth, and a high title. Was she being foolish hoping that the betrothal would come to an end? Did she truly value her own choice so much that she would throw aside something that so many others in society would pursue with everything they had?

"I..." Augusta trailed off, looking into her friend's eyes and knowing that, with Lady Mary, she had to be honest.

"I shall consider what you have said," she agreed eventually as Lady Mary's frown finally lifted completely. "You are right to state that he *is,* in fact, a marquess, and mayhap he is not a match that I should be so eager to thrust aside."

"Might I inquire as to how often you have been in his company?" Lady Mary asked, turning to stand beside Augusta so that she might look out through the ballroom a little better. "Do you know him *very* well? Does he have a difficult personality that makes your eagerness to wed him so displeasing?"

Augusta winced as a knowing look came into Lady Mary's eyes. "I confess that I have not spent any time with him at all," she admitted, "save for our introduction and, thereafter, a country dance." She lifted one shoulder in a half shrug whilst avoiding Lady Mary's gaze. "Perhaps I have been a little hasty."

Lady Mary chuckled and nodded. "Mayhap," she agreed, with a smile that lit up her expression. "He may very well be a very fine gentleman indeed, Lady Augusta, and soon, you will be considered the most fortunate of all the young ladies present in London for the Season."

As much as Augusta did not want to accept this, as much as she wanted to remain determined to make her own choice, she had to admit that Lady Mary had made some valid considerations and she ought to take some time to think through all that had been said. It was not with trepidation but with a sense of curiosity deep within her that she walked through the ballroom with Lady Mary by her side, ready to greet Lord Leicestershire again. There was a little more interest in her heart and mind now, wondering what he would say and how he would appear when he greeted her. With a deep breath, she smiled brightly as she drew near him, her heart quickening just a little as she curtsied.

"Lord Leicestershire," she said, lifting her eyes to his and noting, with a touch of alarm, that there was not even a flicker of a smile touching his lips. "Good evening. How very good to see you again."

Lord Leicestershire frowned, his brow furrowed and his eyes shadowed. "Pardon me, my lady," he said as the other gentlemen he was talking to turned their attention towards both her and Lady Mary. "But I do not recall your name. In fact," he continued, spreading his hands, "I do not think we have ever been acquainted!"

Augusta's mouth dropped open in astonishment, her eyes flaring wide and her cheeks hot with embarrassment as she saw each of the gentlemen looking at her and then glancing at each other with amusement. Lady Mary gaped at Lord Leicestershire, her hand now on Augusta's elbow.

"If you will excuse me," Augusta croaked, trying to speak with strength only for her to practically whisper. "I must..."

"You are due to dance," Lady Mary interjected, helpfully guiding Augusta away from Lord Leicestershire. "Come, Lady Augusta."

Augusta let her friend lead her from the group, feeling utter humiliation wash all over her. Keeping her head low, she allowed Lady Mary to guide her to the opposite side of the room, silently praying that no one else was watching her. Glancing from one side to the other, she heard the whispers and laughter coming from either side of her and closed her eyes tightly, fearful that the rumors and gossip were already starting. For whatever reason, Lord Leicestershire had either chosen to pretend he did not know her or truly had forgotten her, and either way, Augusta was completely humiliated.

CHAPTER THREE

I t had been rather cruel for him to treat Lady Augusta
so, Stephen had to admit, but when he had seen her
from across the ballroom, the memory of how she had
treated him the first time they met had swung back into
his mind with such force that he had felt a surge of anger
and frustration that he could not help himself. Watching
her walk across the ballroom, hanging onto her friend
with her head held low, he had felt a surge of satisfaction
—which was then swiftly followed by a flood of guilt.

Guilt that he had finally managed to remove from
himself without too much difficulty. Life had changed
significantly since he had found himself the Marquess of
Leicestershire, and since his return to society, he had
found himself stepping into a role that he was not at all
used to.

However, last night, he had found himself finally
surrounded by gentlemen and ladies eager to know him
just for himself, rather than to ask questions about any of
his other relations. He had been the center of attention

and, whilst he had convinced himself that he did not *want* nor enjoy such attention, he had found himself becoming more and more pleased with the conversation and the introductions that had been made.

There had been young ladies evidently delighted to be acquainted with him, their blushes making him smile. Gentlemen had been glad to reacquaint themselves with him, although all of them had expressed their sorrow and regret at his brother's passing. Six months was longer than the required time for his mourning period, but Stephen had needed it all, making certain that his mother was comfortable and secure whilst ensuring that he took on everything to do with the estate and understood it thoroughly. His brother had not been the most responsible of men but had, thankfully, not allowed the estate to fall into disrepair. The fields were producing all that was required, and a considerable profit would be his come the harvest. Thus, all that had now been required of him was to return to society and to reacquaint himself with his betrothed.

Stephen grimaced, passing a hand over his eyes as he looked at the papers on his desk, well aware the betrothal agreement had not yet been sent to Lord Elmsworth. He had not felt any particular need to do so, not when he had been in the midst of his grief and confusion, but now that he was back within society, there appeared to be no reason for him to hesitate any longer. And yet, something held him back. Perhaps it was the memory of how Lady Augusta had treated him on their first meeting, or mayhap a new reluctance on his part. A reluctance that was borne from his newfound popularity and status within society. Stephen considered this for a moment and then rose from his chair, wandering towards the window, his hands behind his back as he looked out on the scene below him.

A quiet rap to the door caught his attention, and he turned. "Yes?"

"Lord Dryden has come to call, my lord." The butler came into the room quickly, handing Stephen Lord Dryden's card—but Stephen waved it away.

"Lord Dryden is to be shown in without delay any time he wishes to call," he told the butler, who nodded and scurried away. Within a few moments, Lord Dryden had stepped through the door, his face split with a smile as he looked towards Stephen.

"Lord Leicestershire," he grinned as Stephen welcomed him in. "Thank you for allowing me entrance —me, a humble viscount visiting a marquess."

Stephen laughed wryly and shook his head. "You do yourself a disservice," he said firmly. "My brother might have been inclined towards choosing his acquaintances based on their status and title, but I certainly am not."

Lord Dryden shook his hand firmly. "I am glad to hear it," he said jovially. "Now, I am to usher you from this house and take you at once to Hyde Park." He stepped to one side and gestured to the door. "Shall we go?"

Stephen frowned. "To Hyde Park?" he said, glancing at the large clock on the mantelpiece above the fireplace. "It is the fashionable hour, is it not?"

Lord Dryden grinned. "It will be, very shortly," he agreed with a small shrug. "But that is precisely why I have been told to bring you there. Have you not heard the young ladies of the *ton* speaking of you?" He laughed aloud as Stephen looked away, a little embarrassed. "I was speaking to Lady Wiltshire only last evening, who was most disappointed that her daughter was not able to be introduced to you since she was abed with a headache. Therefore, she practically *forced* me to promise that I would bring you to Hyde Park so that she might introduce you there."

Stephen felt his chest swell with a sense of pride and could not keep the grin from his face. "I see," he replied, still feeling a little abashed, but the sensation fading away a little too quickly. "Then what can I do but agree?" He chuckled to himself as he made his way towards the door, quietly wondering if Lady Wiltshire's daughter would be as beautiful or as charming as the many others he had met last evening. "I confess that, in the past, I have avoided Hyde Park at such a time, for I have never thought I would enjoy it."

Lord Dryden's brows lifted. "You shall enjoy it now," he said with a sardonic smile tipping the corner of his mouth and a strange glint coming into his eye. "I am quite certain of that."

"Good afternoon, Lord Leicestershire!"

"Good afternoon!" Stephen swept into another bow, not quite certain he could recall the name of the young lady curtsying to him. A bead of sweat began to trickle down his neck as he rose from the bow, and he was sure that it did not come solely from being in the warm sunshine. This situation was something entirely new to him, for he struggled desperately to remember the names and situations of all his new acquaintances and yet did not want to make a fool of himself by making his lack of recall obvious.

"And are you enjoying Hyde Park this afternoon?" he asked as the young lady watched him with bright blue eyes, her companion a step behind her, watching her charge carefully. "It is very busy indeed, is it not?"

The young lady smiled back at him, tilting her head just a little and batting her eyelashes in a flirtatious manner. "It is, indeed, Lord Leicestershire," she told him, her voice dripping with syrup. "In fact, I count myself very lucky indeed to have spotted you amongst the crowd. How glad I am that we are able to converse for a time, although I confess that my legs are aching from standing for so long."

Stephen frowned. "Indeed," he murmured, wondering if the young lady needed to sit down, given the heat of the day. "Then might I suggest that you allow yourself a short rest, my lady?" He smiled broadly at her, his heart pounding as he struggled still to recall her name. "I am certain that Lord Dryden would be more than happy to accompany you to a bench or back to your carriage."

There was a moment of silence, only for Lord Dryden to clear his throat hurriedly and to stammer that yes, of course, he would be very glad to accompany the lady to wherever she needed to go. The young lady's eyes narrowed, the blue of her eyes seeming to darken, and she turned on her heel almost at once, her chin in the air, her upset evident.

"Did I say something wrong?" Stephen asked, staring after the lady in confusion. "Why did she—?"

"I believe she did not want *my* company but yours," Lord Dryden said dryly. "You did not know her name now, did you?"

Stephen let out a long sigh and rubbed one hand over his face. "I simply could not recall it," he said honestly. "I wish that I had been able to remember it, but I have had such difficulty in recalling everyone that I have been newly introduced to that I fear I quite forgot her!" His lips caught in a lop-sided smile. "Although I certainly recalled her face. She was very lovely indeed."

Lord Dryden lifted one eyebrow. "I would concur," he said with a gleam in his eye. "Although you need only concern yourself with one young lady this afternoon, I think."

"Oh?" Stephen looked at his friend in confusion. "Which young lady might that be?"

Lord Dryden said nothing, looking back at Stephen steadily as though waiting for him to discover the answer on his own. When Stephen said nothing, Lord Dryden blew out an exasperated breath, his brows knitting.

"I speak of your betrothed," he said, pointedly, throwing up his hands. "I was not present with you last evening, but I have heard precisely what you did to Lady Augusta." His frown deepened and a look of irritation came into his expression, his lips pursed.

"I—I did not mean anything by it," Stephen replied weakly, trying to ignore the stab of guilt that flung itself back into his heart again. "You will recall how she behaved when we were first introduced, I am sure."

"I certainly do," Lord Dryden replied, interrupting Stephen before he could say any more, "but that is not cause to treat her with a callousness that will bring her such a great deal of embarrassment." He shook his head and sighed as though he were correcting a wayward child who struggled to understand him. "You *are* still betrothed, are you not?"

Stephen looked away. "The papers are signed but have not yet been returned to Lord Elmsworth," he said without any intonation in his voice. "I have been intending to do so, but..." Shrugging, he glanced back at Lord Dryden, who had something of a weary look on his face. His brow was furrowed but his eyes were distant and his lips pinched, with his frame appearing a little rigid as though he were battling true frustration. "I will send them to Lord Elmsworth when I am ready to do so."

"Then I hope you intend to tell him such a thing," Lord Dryden muttered, suddenly tuning away from Stephen. "Although, for myself, I think you are being quite foolish."

Stephen opened his mouth to retort, only for Lord Elmsworth to emerge out of the crowd. His steps were purposeful, his eyes fixed on Stephen, and, as Stephen bowed, he noted that Lady Augusta was walking a few steps behind her father, her eyes downcast and her face a little hidden as she kept her head low, her bonnet shielding her from the sun.

"Lord Elmsworth!" Stephen exclaimed as though he

was truly delighted to see the man again. "How do you fare this fine afternoon?"

Lord Elmsworth said nothing for a moment or two, looking into Stephen's face with a sharp eye. Stephen shifted uncomfortably from one foot to the next, wondering if Lady Augusta had told her father what had happened and preparing himself to give some excuse.

"I am glad you know me, at least," Lord Elmsworth said gruffly, turning back to glance at his daughter. "You appear, however, to have forgotten my daughter." He turned a little and gestured for Lady Augusta to step forward. She did so but did not raise her face to his, did not allow her eyes to drift upwards to his. "Given you had such a short meeting before the news came of your poor brother's passing, it is quite understandable that you did not recall her face," Lord Elmsworth continued. "However, I could not permit such a situation to stand, given there is a betrothal between you both." A sudden darkness entered into Lord Elmsworth's features, startling Stephen somewhat. There was a swirling in Lord Elmsworth's eyes now, a tightening of his jaw and a weight to his brows that had sweat trickling down Stephen's back, a fear writhing in his heart that the man knew all too well precisely what Stephen had been doing and why.

"The betrothal," he stammered a little awkwardly. "Yes, of course." He bowed low towards Lady Augusta, heat hitting his face like a wall of flame, burning him from the core. "I must beg your forgiveness, Lady Augusta," he continued, speaking so quickly that his words fell out over each other. "I ought to have remembered you, of course. How could I not?" He spread his hands, licking his lips and finding the air suddenly very dry indeed. "I have met so many new acquaintances since I have taken on my brother's title that I find myself quite overwhelmed."

Lady Augusta finally began to lift her head, but as she did so, Stephen was astonished to note that there was no real sadness there, nor flickering embarrassment. Instead, there was a hardness to her expression, a sharp glint in her eyes that told him he could not feign such a thing to her. Did she know the truth of what he had done? Or was there merely a suspicion that all was not as he liked to make it appear?

"You have not forgotten the betrothal agreement, then?" Lord Elmsworth asked, looking at him with that same flickering suspicion as was in his daughter's eye. "I know you have only just returned to society, Lord Leicestershire, and that to take on such a responsibility as being the Marquess of Leicestershire is a heavy burden indeed, but I had hoped that your previous agreements and arrangements would continue."

"Of course," Stephen found himself saying, wondering if he ought to speak honestly or if he ought to continue to pretend that he had merely been struggling to recall Lady Augusta's face. Looking at Lord Elmsworth, Stephen had the sinking feeling that the gentleman already knew precisely what Stephen was about. Clearing his throat, he spread his hands and chose to speak honestly.

"Lord Elmsworth, I have come back to London and into society, as you have said. However," he continued, daring a glance towards Lady Augusta, who was now watching him with sternness to her gaze, her lips tight and her cheeks filled with color. "However, I have found myself in a different situation from what I am used to."

Lord Elmsworth nodded. "That is to be expected," he said without much indication that he thought that any of this was troubling. "And do you find it a burden to be so sought after within society?"

Stephen opened his mouth to say that yes, he found it *very* difficult indeed, only to close it again. "No, it is not a burden," he answered honestly. "But it is certainly something that I have been struggling to become used to."

This answer seemed to appease Lord Elmsworth somewhat for, as he studied Stephen, the heaviness appeared to leave his expression. His brow was no longer lowered, his eyes no longer hooded and dark. "That is also quite understandable." He looked at Stephen for a few moments longer before spreading out one hand as though he had come to a decision. "Then I shall not press you to return the papers to me, Lord Leicestershire," he said firmly. "So long as I have your word that they will be returned by the end of the Season so that preparations for your marriage can begin."

A swell of relief hit Stephen square in the chest, and he nodded fervently. "But of course, Lord Elmsworth," he said quickly. "I am grateful for your understanding on this matter."

Lord Elmsworth chuckled quietly, putting out his hand for Stephen to shake. "You might be surprised to discover, Lord Leicestershire, that I know full well what it is like to have to go into a new situation when it comes to society and the like," he said with a small smile. "I can still recall just how astonished I was when I first stepped into London as a young gentleman. I cannot imagine how you must be feeling at present, knowing now that your status within the *beau monde* has lifted significantly."

Stephen, awash with relief, allowed himself a quick glance towards Lady Augusta, trying to smile as he did so. She did not look at all like her father. Instead of that lightness of expression, there remained the hard flint in her eyes, the narrowing of her gaze that told him he was not as easily able to explain himself away to her. Her father might believe that Stephen was finding it difficult to adjust to society now that he was a marquess, whereas he felt quite certain that Lady Augusta knew all too well that he was, in fact, enjoying the newfound attention that came his way and did not want to end it all by stating he was now betrothed. Stephen swallowed hard but fixed a smile to his face, forcing it to linger there as he returned his gaze to Lord Elmsworth, who was now smiling and nodding towards him.

"By the end of the Season, I will have the papers returned to you, signed and ready for the marriage preparations to begin," Stephen promised as Lord Elmsworth nodded again. "I thank you for your understanding."

"But of course," Lord Elmsworth replied with a gleam in his eye. "I shall let you go about your business now, Lord Leicestershire." He glanced all about him, a knowing gleam in his eye. "I am certain we are not the only ones eager for your attention. Good afternoon."

"Good afternoon," Stephen echoed, bowing low and only lifting his head completely when he was certain

Lady Augusta had turned away to follow after her father. Guilt and relief mingled together, each battling to take control of his heart, but he forced himself to turn away, wandering through the crowd for only a moment or two before someone else stepped into his path, ready to greet him and to pull him into a conversation.

And within only a few minutes, Lady Augusta and her father had been quite forgotten.

CHAPTER FOUR

Augusta let out a long, slow breath as she walked into the ballroom with her mother just ahead of her. It had been almost a week since she had last seen Lord Leicestershire, and within that week, she had been given ample opportunity to consider her future. Lady Mary, of course, had been a source of almost constant wisdom, and it had been her words and her encouragement that had forced Augusta to reconsider what she had intended to do. This had been coupled with the way Lord Leicestershire had humiliated her by speaking as though he did not recall her, whereas Augusta herself now believed that the gentleman knew *precisely* what he was doing and had done such a thing, mayhap, to bring her much embarrassment. Why he had done so, she could not quite determine, but there was something about Lord Leicestershire that Augusta was beginning to dislike intensely. And yet, within that, there came the knowledge that she had now decided to proceed with the betrothal and that, in a short time, he would be her husband.

Greeting their hosts in an almost mechanical fashion, given her thoughts were so centered on Lord Leicestershire, Augusta walked into the ballroom a little more and tried to force her thinking onto something else—but to no avail. Lord Leicestershire would be there this evening and Augusta intended to ensure that she procured at least one dance from him.

She winced to herself as she recalled just how easily her father had turned from disapproval to understanding when he had spoken to Lord Leicestershire in Hyde Park. As she had turned away from him, walking alongside her father, she had heard her father laugh softly to himself and had not had any hesitation in questioning the reason for his mirth.

Her father had glanced down at her, his expression a little rueful. He had told her that it was clear that, whilst Lord Leicestershire fully intended to continue with the agreement as planned, he was also finding a sense of enjoyment in his new status within society and that he could not begrudge Lord Leicestershire that. Augusta had wanted to protest, to say that *she* found such a thing to be a little upsetting, that she wanted the *ton* to know that she was to marry Lord Leicestershire and that she did not want her betrothed to parade about London as though he were entirely unattached, but the words had died on her lips as her father had chuckled again and then hurried back to towards his acquaintances.

Augusta had, thankfully, found one or two young

ladies to speak with and the rest of the afternoon had passed pleasantly enough, but Augusta had been unable to remove her thoughts from Lord Leicestershire entirely. It had been that way ever since, to the point that she was beginning to fear she might never be free of him again.

"He appears to be doing very well, does he not?"

With a sigh of relief, Augusta pressed Lady Mary's hand, glad for her company. Lady Mary had just stepped out of the shadows, having been waiting for Augusta to arrive and, in the meantime, watching Lord Leicestershire with sharp eyes.

"He does," Augusta agreed, glad that at least Lady Mary knew all that had occurred so that she was able to speak openly to her about it. "I tell myself that there is no reason for my sorrow nor my frustration, and yet there is a part of me that wants to stride across the floor and demand that he send the papers to my father at once." She laughed ruefully, astonished by the sudden tug of sorrow that attempted to pull her heart low. "It is quite ridiculous. Only a few days ago, I imagined that I wanted myself free from him, only to realize now that I would do very well to marry a marquess." Laughing again as Lady Mary nudged her, Augusta smiled. "Thanks to you, of course."

"I have very sage advice indeed," Lady Mary told her, with a small flicker of mirth in her eyes. "Now, I am sure that there is nothing you need worry about. Lord Leicestershire either *does* require a little more time to become used to the idea of matrimony, or else he simply needs time to enjoy the attention that being an unattached marquess brings."

Augusta frowned. "I find that idea to be a little irritating," she answered truthfully, suddenly spotting Lord Leicestershire in the crowd and seeing him laugh heartily at something someone said to him. "I cannot say why, but that feeling is within my heart regardless."

Lady Mary twisted her head around to look away from Augusta towards Lord Leicestershire, evidently seeing the direction of Augusta's gaze. "Then mayhap you ought to attempt to garner some of his attention," she said slowly, looking back at Augusta with a slight widening of her eyes. "Why should you not attempt to know your betrothed a little better, even if you are one of the few who, at present, knows you are engaged?"

A slow flush began to creep up Augusta's neck as she considered this. "What if he pretends he does not recall me again?" she asked, feeling that same twinge of embarrassment. "I am sure he did so purposefully the first time, and I am afraid that he might do so again."

A spark flew into Lady Mary's eyes. "Then why do you not do something similar?" she asked, making Augusta frown heavily. "If he has brought you deliberate embarrassment, then surely there is scope for you to retaliate." She laughed and lifted one shoulder. "That is one way to garner his attention, I am sure!"

Augusta's frown deepened, but she did not immediately ignore or push aside the idea. Even when Lady Mary began to protest that she had been teasing, that she had not meant for Augusta to take such a suggestion seriously, Augusta found herself considering this idea for a good few minutes, her eyes flicking back towards her betrothed before returning to Lady Mary's face.

"It would be childish," she began slowly as Lady Mary nodded fervently. "It would be a little ridiculous even to consider, and yet..."

"No!" Lady Mary protested, her hand now on Augusta's arm. "You must not, Lady Augusta! I was only jesting, truly!"

"But it would force him to notice me," Augusta interrupted before Lady Mary could say more. "It would make it quite clear that I do not believe, as my father does, that he ought to be permitted to enjoy all the attention society brings so that he might laugh, converse, and even *flirt* with the young ladies who come near to him, all eager to fawn over his every remark so that they might have a little hope of becoming his marchioness."

A dull anger began to settle in her stomach, surprising her at the force of her passion as she looked back to Lord Leicestershire, seeing him now bowing over another young lady's hand. "You are right, Lady Mary," she finished as her friend shook her head fervently. "I should do something to gain his attention and to remind him that I am still betrothed to him, even though he has not yet sent the papers to my father."

So saying, she turned towards him and began to make her way across the floor, with Lady Mary having no choice but to trail after her. Augusta walked with purpose, her eyes fixed to Lord Leicestershire who, after a few moments, caught her gaze. She held it tightly, only for him to look away and to laugh at something someone had said, seeming eager to ignore her as he had done once before. Augusta's anger burned hotter and she held her head high as she marched towards him, having no specific intention other than to ensure he greeted her this time.

"Good evening, Lord Leicestershire."

She did not wait for him to bow and certainly did not dip into a curtsy, aware every eye from within the small group was now fixed to her.

"I am afraid you cannot pretend you do not recall me this evening, Lord Leicestershire, since my father has made quite certain to remind you of our previous introduction. And might I introduce my dear friend, Lady Mary."

Lord Leicestershire stared at her for a moment before clearing his throat and stammering awkwardly, shifting his weight from one foot to the next. He bowed stiffly. "Yes, yes, of course, Lady Augusta," he said as a few of his companions exchanged glances. "I must beg your forgiveness for my prior foolishness. Of course, we had been introduced. It was my sluggish mind that was to blame, I think."

"Indeed," Augusta replied dryly, not having any belief in what Lord Leicestershire said. "Well, I am glad that you are able to confess now that the fault was yours, Lord Leicestershire." She arched one eyebrow, looking up into his face and finding the way his eyes darted from here to there to be satisfying in its way. There was an awkwardness that still lingered over him in the way that he shuffled his feet, the way he did not quite meet her gaze, and Augusta felt proud of such a thing. No one else in the small group said a word to her, watching this interaction with great interest and waiting desperately for someone to speak as the tension mounted higher and higher.

"Should—should you like to dance, Lady Augusta?"

Lord Leicestershire's voice was a little higher than before, and he inclined his head as he spoke to her in what she took to be an expression of contrition.

"But of course, Lord Leicestershire," she said, trying to inject a little warmth into her voice. "That is, if there are any remaining!" She laughed as she handed the card to him, waiting for him to look at it before writing his name down. He said nothing, grimacing to himself for a moment or two as though deciding which dance would be the quickest so that he might extract himself from her company just as soon as possible. With a wry twist to his lips, he scribbled his name down and then handed her back the card.

"The country dance," she murmured, a sudden ache hitting her chest as she looked up to see Lord Leicestershire's brow lifting, a sardonic smile on his lips. "I see." It was the dance they had danced together when he had been first introduced to her, the one where they had said not a word to each other all the way through the dance. She had been silent, disliking the fact that her father had thrust her into this betrothal without even talking to her about it first, and Lord Leicestershire, she was sure, had been able to feel the resentment that had been pouring off her in waves. It was no mistake that he had chosen this particular dance for her, and, much to her embarrassment, Augusta felt heat climb up her neck and into her cheeks.

"I look forward to it, Lord Leicestershire," she

murmured, unable to find anything else to say and deciding quickly to turn around and remove herself from him almost at once. Her heart sank as she saw the concerned look in Lady Mary's eyes, hardly able to find the words to express the humiliation she felt.

"I feel as though he has bested me already," she told her friend, reluctantly slipping her dance card back onto her arm. "He has chosen the very dance that we danced when we were introduced, when I am certain he knew very well that I was not at all happy with the engagement." She wrinkled her nose. "I will not pretend that I behaved well, however, for I was not at all contented or welcoming."

Lady Mary sighed and shook her head, although Augusta did not miss the twinkle in her friend's eye, nor the way that her mouth tipped up on one side. She stopped and turned to face her friend whilst Lady Mary put on an entirely innocent expression.

"You think this a little ridiculous, I think," Augusta said firmly. "What advice would you give me then, Lady Mary?"

Lady Mary considered this, not denying that she was filled with mirth, tilting her head to one side for a moment. "I would advise you not to do anything more to either frustrate or irritate him, to step away from your plan to do precisely that—but I fear that my words will fall on deaf ears." She smiled, and Augusta sighed and looked away, knowing that her friend was right. "You will toy with Lord Leicestershire in whatever way you intend, as I fear he will do the very same to you." The light faded from her eyes and she looked at Augusta with concern. "I am not certain that it will lead you towards a happy and contented state of marriage, however."

Augusta thought for a moment, then shrugged. "I will not allow Lord Leicestershire to simply ignore me and delight himself in all the other attention that will certainly come his way," she said decisively. "If I am to be his wife, then I expect him to attempt to show an interest in me that is becoming of a gentleman seeking to know his bride, even if our engagement is not yet known." She lifted her chin, a sense of certainty surrounding her now. "And I will get his attention one way or the other."

As THE MUSIC came to a close, Augusta felt a warm glow of satisfaction settle within her chest as she looked up into Lord Millerton's face, seeing how he smiled at her.

"I thank you for a wonderful dance, Lord Millerton," she said with as much eagerness as she could. "I have always enjoyed the country dance."

Lord Millerton beamed at her. "I was very glad to step in," he said, bowing to her. "What a disappointment that your partner did not come in search of you!"

Augusta sighed dramatically as she rose from her curtsy. "Indeed," she said, making no mention of the fact that she had deliberately placed herself directly across from Lord Leicestershire, with a very large gap between to the two of them so that she might hide away and make quite certain that he could not find her when the time came. "I cannot *think* where Lord Leicestershire would have gone to. Surely he knew that it was time for our dance?" Painting on a mournful expression, she took the proffered arm that Lord Millerton held out to her and began to walk back to the rest of the guests, leaving the dance floor empty for the next dance.

"Lord Leicestershire ought not to have behaved with such inconsideration," Lord Millerton said firmly. "That is not at all becoming."

"Well, I am truly grateful for *your* company," she said, feeling contented with herself. "I thank you, Lord Millerton, for coming to my aid as you did."

"But of course." He let go of her arm and bowed once more, leaving her to stand by Lady Mary, who herself had only just been returned from the country dance. She looked at Augusta sharply, her lips pulled taut and with no need to express the fact that she found what Augusta had done to be somewhat displeasing. Augusta opened her mouth to state that she did not feel any embarrassment, only for Lord Leicestershire to suddenly appear at her side.

"Lady Augusta!" Lord Leicestershire protested, throwing up his hands. "I looked for you, but I could not find you anywhere. And then I see you standing up with another gentleman entirely!"

Augusta blinked rapidly in evident surprise at the sharpness of his tone. "Lord Leicestershire, I hardly think you can hold me responsible for accepting the offer of another gentleman's company for the country dance when you yourself were entirely absent!" She placed her hands on her hips and tilted her head to one side. "I waited and waited, but you did not appear!"

Lord Leicestershire glowered at her. "I tried to seek you out but—"

"There is no need for any such excuses," Augusta interrupted, now holding up one hand, palm outward and towards him. "I have already been humiliated enough. I am only grateful that Lord Millerton stepped in when I needed someone to remove my shame from me." Managing to have a little break in her voice, Augusta looked away as though she was deeply distraught. "Was that your intention, Lord Leicestershire? To offer me the country dance to remind me of my less than welcoming behavior towards you when we first met, only to throw me aside and leave me to stand there alone instead of coming to dance with me as you ought?"

Lord Leicestershire glared at her, his face now a little flushed. "I do not know what game you are playing, Lady Augusta, but it will not wash with me."

"Game?" Augusta's head shot up, all upset gone. "It is not I who is playing a game, Lord Leicestershire, but *you*." She saw his eyes flare and his lips thin but pressed on, speaking her mind without hesitation. "You pretend as though you are not engaged to be married, refusing to give the betrothal papers to my father so that the *ton* does not know of the agreement in any form. Instead, you desire to enjoy yourself during this Season, to lap up all the attention and the interest that comes to you from every direction. You mock me, trying to humiliate me in front of your peers by pretending that we are not introduced, as though I *deserve* such a thing from you."

Lord Leicestershire's eyes darkened, and his brow furrowed. "I do not think I need to remind you, Lady Augusta, of *your* behavior when we first met?"

"And so you think to retaliate?" Augusta spat, her

anger sparking and boiling furiously. "Did you ever even consider that I might not wish for such an arrangement, Lord Leicestershire? That I was struggling with the fact that this betrothal had been made without my parents even considering mentioning it to me?" She saw him look away and felt her stomach turn over. "No, you did not," she continued, seeing him glance towards the floor. "And yet, no matter what I say, you are still determined to do as you please so that you might enjoy the Season in your way, pretending to the *beau monde* that you are quite unattached while knowing full well that it is not so."

For a few moments, Lord Leicestershire said nothing. His eyes were pinned to the floor, his shoulders lifted, and his head lowered. Augusta forced herself to remain silent, her chest rising and falling steadily as she fought to keep control of her composure. She did not know how many others had overheard their conversation, praying that none had given it very much attention, but did not dare look to the right or left, keeping her eyes fixed to Lord Leicestershire.

"You are not the sort of young lady I want as my bride."

Lord Leicestershire's voice was soft, and yet the words he spoke sounded like thunderclaps.

"I will not pretend that I have not signed the agreement, Lady Augusta," he continued slowly dragging his gaze up towards her eyes, "for whilst I have done so, it has not yet been sent to your father." His eyes were like deep pools, hiding all emotion from her and yet holding such a chill that she felt it run down her spine.

"I fully intend to withhold them for as long as I

please," he continued quietly. "I am easily able to convince your father that I need a little more time, but in truth, Lady Augusta, I shall be seeking a way to break the contract without any great difficulties or besmirching of reputations falling on either of us as a consequence."

Augusta sucked in a breath, one hand pressed against her stomach as she stared at Lord Leicestershire, hardly able to believe what was being said. The humiliation that would follow should he manage to extract himself from their agreement was almost more than she could bear.

"I will be polite and considerate towards you, Lady Augusta, for the rest of the Season, of course," Lord Leicestershire finished with a tight smile. "And since I fear that I will struggle to find a way to extricate myself from this agreement, we shall continue to converse and the like, but do not have any expectations or hopes that you will be able to change my mind on this. From what I have seen of you, from what I now understand of your character, I am sorry to say that I do not think you will make me a suitable match, Lady Augusta." He inclined his head and looked away. "Good evening, Lady Augusta."

Augusta watched Lord Leicestershire walk away from her, her feet fastened to the floor as she attempted to take hold of herself. It had come as such a shock that she could barely catch her breath, her chest heaving and her mind swirling with all manner of questions. She felt Lady Mary touch her arm, heard her ask if she was quite all right, but found herself entirely unable to answer. Closing her eyes, Augusta let out a shuddering breath, feeling her future evaporate into nothingness, a dark and empty void now in its place.

"Oh, Mary," she whispered, opening her eyes but finding her vision blurred with unshed tears. "What is it that I have done?"

CHAPTER FIVE

"She made a mockery of me, Dryden."

Lord Dryden said nothing, sitting back in his chair and sipping his brandy without making a single comment. Stephen glowered at his friend and attempted to allow the silence to fill the room, only for the urge to speak again to overwhelm him.

"I mean, she danced with another gentleman and then attempted to place the blame solely on my shoulders!" he continued, throwing himself out of his chair and beginning to march up and down the room. "I had been searching for her, and I am certain, given the look in her eyes, that she had hidden away deliberately." He shook his head, his jaw working. "She attempted to pretend that she was greatly upset but I was not fooled by her theatrics."

Lord Dryden looked at him, a heavy sigh leaving his lips. "This was a little over a sennight ago, was it not?"

Stephen threw up his hands. "And yet I am still irritated by it all!" he exclaimed. "I have seen her a good many times over the last few days, at almost every social occasion we have attended, and each time, she had turned from me and barely looked me in the eye. It is quite ridiculous."

With what was another wearied sigh, Lord Dryden tipped his head and considered this. "What Lady Augusta did in dancing the country dance with another gentleman may have been nothing more than a childish attempt to humiliate you in the same way that you idiotically chose to mortify her by pretending that you were not acquainted with her," he pointed out, making Stephen turn away, a little displeased.

"You did not consider that, I gather," Lord Dryden said, one eyebrow lifted questioningly. "Goodness, you have made something of a rash decision, if I might be permitted to say so."

Stephen grimaced, aware of the flicker of irritation in his heart over being berated by his friend.

"I do not need to consider it," he said, a little tartly. "I have made a decision based on what I know of the lady, and thus, I have decided that she is not the sort of young lady that would suit."

Lord Dryden snorted and rolled his eyes, turning Stephen's irritation to anger. "I do not see what makes you think that you can react in such a fashion," he continued, a little more loudly now. "You state that you know Lady Augusta a little better than I, but that does not mean that I cannot make a wise decision based on my impression of her."

"What do you know of her, exactly?" Lord Dryden asked, clearly not at all affected by Stephen's sharp words. "She may have made a poor impression upon you at the start but that does not mean that you know her at all." One shoulder lifted in a half shrug. "And if I may be as so bold as to say, it is not as though you have made an excellent impression on her either."

Stephen opened his mouth to retort, only to close it again at the knowing look that came to Lord Dryden's eye. He could not deny that fact as much as he would like to.

"I have made my decision," he said smartly. "No matter what you suggest or what you lay out before me, I have no intention of going back on my word. Lady Augusta will think me truly foolish if I do such a thing."

Lord Dryden shook his head and sighed as though Stephen were being truly ridiculous but, much to Stephen's relief, saying nothing further.

"Now," Stephen said, a little more firmly. "Are we to go to this afternoon tea at Lady Whitakers' or would you prefer to berate me a little more whilst enjoying what is a most excellent brandy?" He chuckled at the considered look on Lord Dryden's face, ignoring the fact that he still felt uncomfortable about his decision regarding Lady Augusta. He told himself that he had made his mind up and that there was no need to discuss it further, even though there was now a slight twinge of guilt thanks to Lord Dryden.

"I suppose we should, yes," Lord Dryden muttered, casting an almost mournful look towards the brandy in the corner of the room. "That is quite excellent brandy, I must say."

With a roll of his eyes, Stephen gestured for his friend to precede him from the room. Lady Whitaker's afternoon tea was sure to be a spectacular occasion, for she had a very large townhouse and, with it, at the back of the house, beautiful gardens that were the envy of a good many within the *ton*. With a rich husband who seemed to do very little other than remain at his estate and allow his wife to do as she pleased, Lady Whitaker threw wonderful events, and it was a privilege to be invited. Stephen had not ever been asked to attend before, of course, given he had been the lowly brother of a marquess, but now, he was eagerly expected.

"I must ask you something," Lord Dryden began as they hurried down the staircase, ready to collect their hat and gloves before making their way to the waiting carriage. "That young lady who is friends with Lady Augusta." His eyes darted away for a moment, clearing his throat as he sat down in the carriage. "I do not recall being acquainted with her."

For a moment, Stephen found himself lost for words, surprised to hear his friend speak so. "I believe her name is Lady Mary," he said slowly, noting the slight flush to his friend's face. "I have only met her the once but not spoken to her at any great length." He narrowed his eyes, keeping his gaze fixed onto Lord Dryden, who was now steadfastly looking out of the window. "Is there a particular reason as to—"

"I think her a very handsome creature," Lord Dryden said, turning his head sharply to look straight back at

Stephen without any sign of embarrassment. "And I should like to know her better."

Stephen blinked in surprise, not quite certain how to respond to such a remark. "I see."

"I am inclined towards finding a suitable wife," Lord Dryden said, a gleam of mirth in his eye. "After all, seeing the mess you are making of things makes me all the more inclined to prove that it *can* be done without any great difficulty whatsoever!"

Stephen could not help but laugh as Lord Dryden grinned in a most boyish fashion, turning his head to one side and looking out of the window once more. They sat in silence for the remainder of the journey, their thoughts their only company until, finally, they arrived at Lady Whitaker's abode.

"I AM SO VERY glad to see you here this afternoon, Lord Leicestershire."

Stephen smiled down at Lady Whitaker, feeling his chest swell with the look of delight in Lady Whitaker's eyes. Finally, they were all looking at him, glad that he was a part of society rather than being ignored. "I thank you for your *kind* invitation," he replied, bowing at the waist as Lady Whitaker giggled like a young debutante, her eyes flashing with evident pleasure at his remark. "I am delighted to be here."

Lady Whitaker laughed again and, as she turned to welcome him into the room, he felt her hand on his arm, running from his wrist up to his elbow in a slow motion that sent a slight prickling sensation all through him—and not one that was in any way pleasant. His smile began to die away as he looked at the gathered crowd, wondering if he would be able to remove himself from Lady Whitaker's grip quickly.

"Ah, I can see the doors to the gardens are open," he commented, making to step forward, only for Lady Whitaker to hold him back.

"They are quite wonderful," Lady Whitaker told him, one eyebrow arching slowly. "I do hope that we might meet there later, so I can show you some of my favorite spots."

Stephen cleared his throat, forcing his smile back to life as he glanced down towards her. "I—yes, Lady Whitaker," he said hastily, thinking that if he agreed, he would soon be able to extract himself from her. "That would be quite lovely."

"Good," Lady Whitaker purred, finally releasing his arm so that he could step away. "Until later this afternoon then, Lord Leicestershire."

Moving away quickly, Stephen let his gaze brush across the room, making his way towards the French doors and feeling as though the heat and the warm air from the room was a little oppressive.

"Lord Leicestershire, how very good to see you!"

He stopped hastily just as a young lady, together with a lady he presumed to be her mother, swiftly stepped in front of him.

"You will forgive my impropriety, Lord Leicestershire, but I believe you are already acquainted with my daughter and I *had* to come to make myself acquainted with you also." The lady smiled and glanced towards her daughter, whom, Stephen realized with an inner groan, was the very same young lady he had met previously. A young lady whose name he still could not quite recall. When he had last seen her, he had made the foolish mistake of suggesting that Lord Dryden take her back towards her carriage when it was quite clear—according to Lord Dryden—that she had sought Stephen's company.

Evidently, she was not a young lady inclined towards giving up.

"I am very glad to meet you," he said to the as-yet unnamed older lady, taking a few moments to drop into an ornate bow. "And good afternoon to you also." He bowed again towards the young lady, hoping that she did not notice his reluctance to use her name. "Might you introduce me to your mother?"

The young lady's gaze narrowed slightly, no smile on her lips as she looked at him steadily. He returned her gaze with a smile and a hopeful look, which, thankfully, was returned by the lady turning to her mother and gesturing towards her.

"This is my mother, Viscountess Villiers," the young lady said as the lady dropped into a most elegant curtsy. "Thank you for taking the time to greet us, Lord Leicestershire."

He smiled at her again, but still, the young lady did not return it. "But of course," he said with a grand bow. "I am very glad to have made your acquaintance."

"I do hope you will take my daughter for a short turn about the grounds," Lady Villiers said without hesitation. "I would do so myself, of course, but I confess I am quite weary." She waved a hand as though gesturing at the heat all around them. "It is the warm summer days that bring a tiredness to my limbs that I simply cannot avoid," she finished dramatically. "And yet, my dear girl wants desperately to walk about the gardens so that she might take them in, in all their beauty." Light blue eyes, framed by dark eyelashes, batted at him as though she were a young lady trying to encourage the interest of a gentleman. "I would be *most* grateful and, of course, I will watch you both carefully from my present situation so that there will be not even a hint of impropriety."

Stephen cleared his throat, seeing how the young lady watched him with hard eyes, her mother's expression expectant, and felt cornered. He had no other choice but to take her, finding a bead of sweat running down his back as he tried desperately to remember the lady's name. "But of course," he said, smiling at her brightly as he offered her his arm. "I should be very glad of your company."

"I thank you," Lady Villiers said at once, a hand on his arm for just a moment. "You are very kind indeed, Lord Leicestershire."

He smiled tightly, trying to rid himself of the tension that flooded him. "But of course," he said with another quick bow. "Shall we?" He offered the young lady his arm, turning her towards the French doors and beginning to make his way towards it. The lady walked quietly, no words on her lips and no expression of delight in her eyes. Were he merely observing her, he would state that she did not want to be where she was at present, clearly disliking his company and perhaps wishing she were elsewhere.

"It is a fine day, indeed," he said, a little more loudly than he had intended as they stepped out of doors. "The sky has not even a single cloud within it."

The lady said nothing in response but kept her head held at such an angle that her bonnet kept the sun from her face, not looking up to the sky as he had done. They began to walk through the gardens, with Stephen nodding and smiling at various acquaintances as they did so. His forehead began to bead as he continued to walk, wondering at the strange quietness of the lady beside him and beginning to be afraid that she knew his dilemma.

"My mother is very forward." The lady's voice was tight, her eyes darting up towards him as he dared to glance at her. "She was very eager to make your acquaintance."

"I was very glad to be able to do so," he told her, not at all truthfully. "Do you have any other social occasions that you will both be attending soon?"

The young lady looked up at him, evidently surprised at his question. "Yes," she said slowly. "We will be going to Lord Sombes' ball this evening, and then to a soiree tomorrow," she said as though trying to work out his reasons for speaking so. "And you?"

He shrugged. "I confess that I have had so many invitations that I struggle to recall which ones I have accepted and what I am to attend," he said with a slight air to his words. "My butler and my valet usually take care of all such things. I am sure I will be duly informed when I return home this evening as to what I am to attend next." He laughed at this remark, with the young lady finally allowing herself a small smile. "I am certain we will be able to see each other again very soon."

"Indeed." The young lady looked surprised, then her smile broadened. "I would be very glad of your company at any time you wish to seek me out," she said as Stephen smiled to himself, thinking of just how much things had changed for him. He had never once had such interest in him as he did at present, had never had such eagerness in a lady's eyes as she had looked up at him. Yes, of course, there was some unwanted attention—as there was with Lady Whitaker—but to see such delight in a young lady's eyes when he sought out her company was quite wonderful indeed.

"Ah."

A slight uncomfortable exclamation had him brought back to the present, his eyes focusing on Lord Dryden, who was walking with Lady Mary and Lady Augusta. His throat began to tighten as he looked from one to the next, trying not to avoid Lady Augusta's gaze.

"Good afternoon, Lord Leicestershire," Lady Mary said, bobbing a curtsy. "I do hope you are enjoying this afternoon so far."

"I am, I thank you," he answered, aware of how Lord Dryden had Lady Mary's hand resting on his arm and marveling at just how quickly he had managed to procure the lady's attention. "Lady Augusta, are these gardens not quite lovely?"

Lady Augusta's eyes glazed over, and she looked away as though looking about the gardens when he was certain that her main reason for doing so was simply to avoid looking into his face. "They are quite marvelous, yes," she said, her voice soft but with no expression of delight in her features. Finally, her eyes turned back towards him, only to rest on the lady on his arm. Her eyes flared for a moment, evidently taking in his closeness to her before Lady Augusta looked away, her cheeks beginning to flood with color.

"I must beg your pardon," Lady Mary said quickly, giving Stephen a quick smile so as to cover for Lady Augusta. "I fear I do not know your acquaintance." She bobbed a quick curtsy towards his company. "Might I beg an introduction?"

Stephen's mouth went dry as he swallowed hard, his throat clogging as he tried to find something to say. He could not make an introduction when he did not know the lady's name! It was deeply mortifying and try as he might, he could not find something to say.

"Lady Mary," he rasped, not quite certain how he was to continue, glancing at Lady Augusta only to see that she was looking directly at him now, a look of curious puzzlement in her eyes. "I must apologize for my lack of propriety." Desperately, he looked to Lord Dryden, who frowned, clearly uncertain as to what was troubling Stephen. "Lord Dryden, I presume you also lack an introduction?"

Lord Dryden nodded slowly, his brow furrowed and his brows knitting together. "I fear I am as Lady Mary is," he said with a very quick smile towards Stephen's companion. "If you would be so kind, Lord Leicestershire?"

Stephen nodded, his breath coming quick and fast as

he struggled to think of what to say. His mind scrambled, running over every name he could think of, trying desperately to recall something that would catch something in his mind.

"Miss Trevelyan, is it not?"

His breath caught as Lady Augusta took a small step forward, her eyes bright and a broad smile on her face that did not betray anything other than the enjoyment of the moment. "I must apologize. I thought that we were all already introduced."

"Not at all," Miss Trevelyan said quickly, glancing up towards Stephen, who was so overcome with relief that he felt a little faint. "I am sure Lord Leicestershire will be more than able to do the introductions."

"But of course," Stephen said, his voice hoarse and his chest tight. Quickly, he introduced Miss Trevelyan as the daughter of Viscount Villiers, watching as Lady Mary curtsied and Lord Dryden bowed. "And I believe you are already acquainted with Lady Augusta."

There was that same, broad smile settled on Lady Augusta's face, but as he looked into her eyes, he saw the way she looked back at him. There was something in her gaze, something that told him that she understood precisely what his difficulty had been and had stepped in so that he would not embarrass himself and have gossip flung about London because of him.

"Might you care to join us for a short time?" Lady Mary asked as Miss Trevelyan quickly stepped away, apparently quite eager to continue a conversation with her new acquaintances. "These gardens are quite magnificent, even though they are not overly large."

"I could not agree more," Miss Trevelyan said, leaving Lady Augusta and Stephen standing together, a strange awkwardness now beginning to flood the space between them. Lady Augusta did not meet his eyes, turning her whole body slightly and beginning to trail after the other three, although she did linger behind.

"Lady Augusta." Stephen reached out and caught her arm, with Lady Augusta turning almost at once, her eyes fastened to the ground. This was a new Lady Augusta, a side of her he had not seen before. There was no sense now that she was pretending, play-acting a piece of herself to manipulate his emotions in any way. Had he broken her spirit? In choosing to step away, had he damaged her in some way?

"Lady Augusta," he said quietly, looking into her face and finding within himself a very strong desire for her to lift her head and gaze back at him. "Lady Augusta, I cannot thank you enough for what you did."

Lady Augusta did not smile, and there was no intonation in her voice as she spoke. "I could see from your expression that you were having some difficulty in recalling your companion's name."

"Yes, but you could have left me to struggle," he told her, feeling his sense of confusion beginning to grow as he looked at her steadily. "Why did you not?"

Finally, Lady Augusta lifted her eyes to his, a calmness within the emerald green. "I am not callous, Lord Leicestershire," she stated, speaking to him as though he did not know her in any way, shape or form. "I will not pretend that I have behaved impeccably towards you since our very first introduction. I have perhaps been foolish and certainly very upset over certain..." She stopped, shaking her head as though to remind herself to remain silent, before closing her eyes tightly. "That is to say, Lord Leicestershire, that I have no desire to bring you any pain or embarrassment any longer." Opening her eyes, she looked at him again, one shoulder lifted. "You have made it quite clear that you intend to put an end to the agreement between our families, Lord Leicestershire, and I am not the sort of lady who is eager to punish you for it. I helped you because I had compassion for your struggle."

"But why?" The question came to his lips without his intention, stepping closer to look into her eyes, finding that what Lord Dryden had said was now quite clear. He did *not* know who she was, did not understand anything about her. She had made a poor impression, and he had been just as foolish, it seemed. Overly hasty, mayhap.

"Why should I not be considerate?" she asked him as though it was the most understandable answer in all the world. "Even though I see the truth of your character, the true reason behind your decision to try to end our betrothal, you will not find me cruel."

That had him stopping dead in his tracks as he looked at her hard, his brow puckered and a surge of nervousness in his stomach. His eyes fixed to hers, his words tainted with a bitterness that was nothing more than a defense against her response. "And what sort of truth do you believe you see in me, Lady Augusta?"

Lady Augusta smiled softly as if she were entirely unaffected by the hardness of his words and the angry expression on his face. "I have seen that your new title has brought you a recognition that you never have experienced," she said quietly, her words flinging into him like hard arrows. "Society seeks you out like a cat hunting its prey—but you, it seems, remain entirely unaware of the danger."

"What danger?" he exclaimed, flinging his arms up before realizing that he was speaking a little too loudly. "If you are suggesting that enjoying all that society has to offer is problematic, Lady Augusta, then I can tell you without a doubt that there is nothing wrong about such a thing!"

She looked at him then, no words passing her lips but allowing silence to pass between them. It stole some of his anger as it passed, his shoulders dropping as he closed his eyes for a moment, dragging in air.

"You are quite correct, I am sure," she told him, her tone gentle, but a slight twist to her lips that told him she did not fully believe him. "I heard all about your character and your nature when we were first introduced, Lord Leicestershire. I have seen you changed now." She gestured to the other guests. "You revel in all of this. You like the attention that comes to you now that you have a high title and, most likely, increased wealth." Again, she lifted one shoulder in a small shrug. "Mayhap that is why you wish to end our betrothal. I cannot say for certain, but I am quite sure that you do not see society's attention for what it truly is."

Her words wormed into his heart, but he shook his head, looking away from her as though doing so would clear the angst that her words had brought him. Before he could respond, Lady Augusta smiled and turned away. "Good evening, Lord Leicestershire."

There was nothing he could say as he looked after her, his jaw working furiously until, finally, he turned on his heel and strode back through the gardens.

CHAPTER SIX

Her heart had been heavy of late, Augusta had to admit. Ever since Lord Leicestershire had told her that he intended to find a way to end their betrothal—even though that in itself might be difficult—she had found herself increasingly sorrowful. It was as though the very thing she wanted had been taken away from her, even though she knew full well that she had attempted, as best she could, to gain this very situation. She had *wanted* her freedom, had yearned for the opportunity to bring things to a close between herself and Lord Leicestershire, believing that she would be able to find a much better match for herself. Now, however, she had come to realize that there was no one better than Lord Leicestershire, even if she did find him to be quite changed due to society's renewed interest in him.

She sighed and let her fingers run along the spines of the books that sat out on the shelf before her, not taking even a minute interest in the names written there. She had thought coming to the bookshop in search of something new to read would be of help, assisting her in clearing her mind, only for her thoughts to quadruple in the quiet silence of the shop.

Augusta sighed again and resisted the urge to lean heavily against the shelf and close her eyes in both sorrow and frustration. With a heaviness still lingering, she continued further down the shop until she reached the end, noting that her mother was still near to the front, evidently distracted by something she had found there. The shop itself was very quiet indeed, perhaps because the day was fine and that most of the *ton* were eager to be seen out and about rather than hiding themselves away. Augusta was glad to step into a place of refuge, knowing that this evening would be one of relief also since they were to attend the theatre with Lady Mary and her mother. There would be very little chance of her seeing Lord Leicestershire, and even less an opportunity to converse with him.

She grimaced, aware that even a few words shared between them brought her a level of pain and frustration. When she had stepped in to rescue him from his dilemma with Miss Trevelyan, she had done so knowing that their conversation thereafter might be a difficult one —and it had certainly proved to be so.

Not that she regretted speaking her mind, she considered, picking up a book and opening it as though she were interested in what was inside. She had seen the difference in Lord Leicestershire's character and had spoken her mind. The way society was pulling him in, holding onto him with greedy fingers as they each tried to make him believe that their interest in him was genuine...she had seen such behavior before. Now that Lord Leicestershire held the title and had a great fortune, all anyone wanted from him was a closeness that would be beneficial to themselves.

"This evening?" There came a quiet little chuckle that had Augusta's hair standing on end. "It will bring him a good deal of embarrassment, I must say."

Augusta froze, the book still in her hand even though she had not read a single word. She frowned to herself, noting that the people who were speaking quietly had not come around to where she now stood. This part of the bookshop was very quiet indeed, with long, heavy, and freestanding bookshelves, which hid Augusta's form from them almost entirely. Should they round the bookshelf, however, they would see her almost at once and she did not want that.

"This will only be the beginning," came the second voice, sounding almost delighted at whatever dark intentions they had. "If there is more, if I find even a moment where he brings even a hint of shame to me, then I shall repay him tenfold."

Shivering—not from the cold but from the malevolence that now filled the lady's voice, Augusta made to move away, only to hear a familiar name being spoken.

"Leicestershire is a fool," said the first voice. "You will easily be able to bend him to your will."

"I do hope so," came the second voice with a hint of resigned sigh deep within it, as though she found the prospect of whatever she intended to do to be quite wearying. "Let us hope it does not take a good deal of time either."

A quiet laugh sent a *frisson* of horror down Augusta's spine and she turned her head away from the end of the bookshelf, wondering if she ought to remain quite still or attempt to hurry back to the other end of the bookshop to where her mother stood. Her heart began to pound furiously as beads of sweat formed at her temples, her indecision making her a little afraid. Another set of footsteps drew near, and Augusta closed her eyes, forcing her breathing to remain as regular as she could. She did not want to be discovered eavesdropping, particularly when she had been attempting to remove her thoughts from Lord Leicestershire. Hearing skirts swishing, Augusta closed her eyes and bent her head low as though she were looking at the book with great interest. She heard some quiet murmurings, unable to make out what was being said with snatches of words coming to her ears. There were three of them now, she was sure, but did not recognize any voices, given they all spoke so quietly.

"During the interval, I presume?"

The agreement that followed had Augusta's head twisting around, such was the vehemence in the lady's voice. There had been a murmur about retribution, as though Lord Leicestershire had done something of great foolishness or wickedness, which Augusta found hard to believe. And thereafter, there had come a few more moments of conversation, which Augusta could not make out at all, only for the conversation to come to a close. One set of footsteps hurried away, the door opening and closing behind the first. Augusta was forced to wait for another few torturous minutes until, finally, she heard the other two ladies, still murmuring quietly, make their way to the door, leaving her standing alone at the end of the bookshop, her heart pounding furiously.

What was she to do? She had no need to protect Lord Leicestershire from anything, and yet these two ladies clearly had the intention to bring him either mortification or damage to his reputation. She could not imagine what he had done to deserve such treatment but felt the burden of responsibility settle in her soul regardless. She could not leave him as he was, unaware and uninformed about what might occur this evening. She had to tell him, had to speak to him to ensure that he knew something untoward might occur that could damage him in some way.

Will he even listen to you? Will he be glad that you came to call?

A vision of his face as she had seen it last rose before her eyes, and she winced, recalling just how angry he had been, how his blue eyes had darkened, swirling with the great and terrible storm that she had awakened within him. She had not allowed him to respond to her, had not let him say even a single word in response but had stepped away from him, letting her final words linger in the hope that he might, in the end, consider what she had said.

He certainly would *not* be inclined to listen to her again now. Besides which, she could not simply call on him unexpectedly! It was not the done thing, and most likely, he would already be engaged, and she could not bear the thought of making polite conversation when her heart was already so heavy.

"Augusta?"

Her mother's bright voice shattered the quietness around Augusta, and she hurried forward, a little nervous that the ladies who had been speaking together would, by now, have heard her mother calling and would know that she had been listening to what had been said. However, as she reached her mother, who was standing with an impatient look in her eyes, her mouth pulled taut and one hand to her hip, Augusta was relieved to see the door to the bookshop swinging closed with what she hoped was the two ladies exiting the shop.

"There you are," Lady Elmsworth said, waving a hand. "I thought I had lost you in the depths of this shop." She took some of the hardness from her words by smiling at Augusta, who handed her mother the book she had picked up some time ago, even though she had not even managed to look at the title.

"Did you see two ladies leave only a few moments ago, Mama?" Augusta asked, glancing behind her mother's shoulder. "Did you recognize either of them?"

Lady Elmsworth let her gaze drift over Augusta's features for a moment, evidently a little displeased with what she saw there. "No, I did not," she said, a slight frown on her features. "Although yes, I did see them depart. Why do you ask?" Her frown deepened as she continued to watch Augusta, who was, by now, trying to come up with some excuse as to why she wanted to know who the ladies were. "Do you wish to become acquainted with them?"

"No, indeed," Augusta answered quickly, her mind still scrambling for ideas. "It is only that...only that one of them was talking excitedly about a book she had been told to she *must* read but when it came time for them to depart, she had not yet found it." She shrugged and gestured to the book her mother held. "I found it only a moment too late."

"I see," Lady Elmsworth murmured, looking down at the book. "I must confess, I am surprised that any young lady would be eagerly searching for a book about the history of Brunswick." She arched one eyebrow and held it out to Augusta, whose only response was to shrug and look away, her cheeks scalding as she prayed her mother would accept what was said. There was another moment of hesitation, only for Lady Elmsworth to sigh and mutter something under her breath, just as Augusta dared to look back at her.

"Do you wish to purchase this?" Lady Elmsworth asked, with a hint of humor in her voice, her eyes dancing as Augusta looked up in surprise. "I am sure that the young lady who was searching for such a book was, most likely, interested in a gentleman who hails from Brunswick and thus, wished to acquaint herself with the history of it as best she could." A laugh escaped her, and Augusta joined in at once, feeling a swell of relief lift her chest. "Unless you particularly wish to acquaint yourself with all that Brunswick offers, might you place this back where you found it?"

"At once," Augusta murmured, taking the book from her mother and hurrying back to where she had picked it up, glad that her mother had accepted such an excuse without a great deal of consideration or confusion. Setting the book back in its place, she hurriedly found a novel that she had not read before and brought it to the proprietor, who quickly added it onto the purchase that Lady Elmsworth herself had made.

"I thank you," Augusta said quietly as she and her mother exited the bookshop, the parcel of books swinging deftly from her hand. "And Mama, I know we are due to call at the dressmakers, but might we return home?" She gave her mother a hopeful look, whilst at the same time attempting to appear quite weary. "I am very tired and should like to rest before the theatre this evening."

This did not appear to upset Lady Elmsworth in any way, even though Augusta had expected her to be so. "But of course, I quite understand," came the reply. "I too am a little tired and would be glad of the rest, although I think Lady Newfield is hoping to call this afternoon also."

"I am sure I shall manage a small cup of tea with her," Augusta said firmly, determined that, once she returned home, she would set about writing to Lord Leicestershire. He *had* to know what was about to occur, even if she did not know the specific details so that he could guard himself most carefully this evening. All Augusta could do was pray that he would receive her notes and read them without delay so that this evening would not bring about the end of Lord Leicestershire's most excellent reputation.

"You look quite lovely this evening, Lady Augusta."

Augusta did not smile, her hand looping through Lady Mary's as she pulled her back gently. "I am greatly concerned," she told her friend, seeing how the smile slipped from Lady Mary's face almost at once. "Perchance this afternoon, I heard something that I am greatly fearful over." Briefly, she explained to Lady Mary what she had overheard, Lady Mary's eyes widening in both horror and upset, clearly as upset as Augusta was about what could soon occur to the gentleman.

"And you seek this evening to tell him so that he remains on his guard?"

"I have written to him already this afternoon," Augusta told her, her desperation rising. "In fact, I wrote to him on three occasions, given I had no response to my first, nor to my second note. The third was sent with the servant told to wait until a reply was given, but after waiting for a full hour, he returned to me having been informed that no reply would be given."

"Goodness!" Lady Mary exclaimed, her eyes wide, one hand pressed to her heart. "What are you to do?"

"I do not know," Augusta replied heavily. "I have tried my hardest to inform him of what is to occur, but I cannot tell if he has even read what I have written to him." Sighing, she tried to paste on a bright smile as they entered the theatre, aware there were a good many *ton* present this evening who would be, she was sure, prepared to find even the smallest piece of gossip they could fling about amongst themselves. She did not want anyone to note that she appeared distressed for most likely, something would be surmised as to the reason for her distress and rumors would soon abound.

"Then you must speak to him directly."

Augusta shook head almost at once. "I cannot," she

said quickly. "I think I have told you of what was passed between us the last time we spoke." Wincing, she did not dare glance at her friend. "He was not particularly pleased with me."

Lady Mary let out a long breath. "And this is now why you think that he has not responded to your notes," she said in understanding. "That is nothing but foolishness on his part, however."

"Be that as it may, it does not detract from the fact that he is still in danger from whatever it is these ladies intend," Augusta replied as Lady Mary led her towards their box. "What must I do?"

Lady Mary stopped dead, turning to face Augusta with what appeared to be a slight flush to her cheeks. Lifting her chin, she put on a quick smile that did not quite reach her eyes, leaving Augusta all the more suspicious. "I will speak to Lord Dryden if you think that would be of any assistance?"

Augusta hesitated, remembering how Lord Dryden and Lady Mary had been first introduced and then had conversed for such a long time that it had been very difficult to pry Lady Mary away from him. Lord Dryden had been more than interested in furthering his acquaintance with the lady, as far as Augusta was concerned, to the point that she hoped something might soon develop between her friend and Lord Dryden, who, by all accounts, was a decent gentleman with a suitable fortune and an excellent estate.

"You are to see Lord Dryden this evening?" she asked, unable to help the grin that appeared on her face as Lady Mary blushed and dropped her gaze. "When?"

Lady Mary waved a hand as though it was of little importance. "I am aware of where his box is situated," she told Augusta, who arched one eyebrow high. "Do not look at me with such interest in your eyes, Lady Augusta. It is quite reasonable for a young lady to know such things."

Augusta could not help but chuckle. "Of course," she said with another broad smile. "But I must ask, Lady Mary, whether or not you have ever *joined* Lord Dryden in his box?" It had been a few days since Lady Mary and Lord Dryden had first met, and Augusta did not know what had occurred between her friend and that particular gentleman since then. "Have you been here with him?"

Again, Lady Mary flapped one hand and let out what Augusta was sure was meant to be a sigh of exasperation, which only made her laugh aloud again. When Lady Mary began to stammer an explanation, it was all Augusta could do to remain silent, her smile and laughter being forced away until her friend could speak.

"Lord Dryden is expecting me in the interval," she finished as Augusta nodded, pressing her lips together tightly so that she would not ask any further questions of her friend. "We could walk there together now, in search of him?"

With a quick glance behind her to where both her mother and Lady Mary's mother stood talking to a small group of acquaintances, including Lady Newfield. Augusta nodded. "We must make great haste, however," she said, hurriedly. "The play will be starting soon, and I do not think my mother would be at all pleased if I were to be absent without her express agreement."

Lady Mary nodded, darting a glance over Augusta's shoulder before she took her hand and began to hurry away.

～

"Lord Dryden—oh!"

Augusta dropped into a curtsy as quickly as she could, hiding her embarrassment at seeing Lord Leicestershire standing there, clearly having been in deep conversation with Lord Dryden. The air seemed to fill with astonishment, with both gentlemen staring at the ladies for a prolonged moment before they quickly got to their feet, pushing themselves from the chairs, before bowing low.

"Lady Mary, Lady Augusta," Lord Dryden said, his voice faltering with evident confusion as he looked from one to the other. "Good evening."

Augusta took a deep breath as Lady Mary murmured a greeting, fixing her gaze to Lord Leicestershire and seeing how his brow furrowed deeply as he looked back at her.

"You will think me most impertinent, Lord Dryden, but I came in search of you to seek your aid and your insight into an important matter."

Lord Dryden's frown deepened. "Oh?"

"It was to do with Lord Leicestershire, in fact," she continued, her eyes now finding Lord Leicestershire's face and seeing the surprise that etched itself into his features. His eyes flared, but his brows knitted as he looked at her steadily, his mouth pulled taut with no words of greeting resting on them.

"Then it is very good that you came to find me when you did," Lord Dryden said warmly, perhaps aware of the frostiness that came rolling from Lord Leicestershire's shoulders. "For, as you can see, Lord Leicestershire is present with me."

"Indeed." Augusta tilted her head and looked at Lord Leicestershire, one brow arched. "I must ask you directly then, Lord Leicestershire, whether or not you have received any notes from me this afternoon?" She watched him closely, trying to find any flicker in his otherwise impassive face, only for him to return her steady gaze with one of her own. "I wrote three times to you this afternoon, Lord Leicestershire."

"*How* unfortunate," came the reply, which Augusta was sure held a touch of sarcasm. "I was quite absent this afternoon, Lady Augusta." From the way Lord Dryden's head swiveled around to look at Lord Leicestershire, Augusta was certain that such a thing was not at all true but knew she could not say so.

"It is of great importance, Lord Leicestershire," Lady Mary interjected, her voice soft but her words filled with eagerness. "She has overhead some dreadful remarks from two ladies who seek to—"

"Whilst I am sure that Lady Augusta's ability to eavesdrop is more than a little pronounced, I have no need for her involvement in any of my matters," Lord Leicestershire interrupted, sending a cold shiver down Augusta's spine, her eyes burning as she felt shame drip down onto her shoulders as though his words had flung such an emotion over her head. "Although I thank you for your concern."

There was nothing but silence now, a silence that was both heavy and oppressive. Augusta's heart had tumbled to the floor, her eagerness to help Lord Leicestershire evaporating in a moment. He had not forgiven her for speaking so honestly to him, then, and was quite determined to put distance between them. Even though her father still believed that their betrothal was to go ahead, Augusta was now all the more convinced that Lord Leicestershire was doing just as he had promised and was now seeking to discover a way to remove himself from her entirely. He was setting a distance between them that she did not think could ever be overcome now.

"How dare you?"

Much to her surprise, Lady Mary stepped forward, one finger pointed out towards Lord Leicestershire, her face the color of holly berries on a cold winter's day. Her whole body was taut, her shoulders lifted and her finger now pressing lightly against Lord Leicestershire. "How dare you speak so, Lord Leicestershire?" she demanded as Augusta watched her friend in shock. "She has overheard something that concerns you and is afraid for your reputation. In her fear, she has come to you to tell you of what she has overheard, hoping that you will take great care to watch your step, only for you to dismiss her without consideration!" Shooting a glance back towards Augusta, Lady Mary swung her head back around towards Lord Leicestershire, a groove forming between her eyebrows as she frowned hard, lines in her forehead deepening as her anger tightened her frame all the more. "Whether or not your betrothal is to continue—yes, you need not look so astonished, I am well aware of what you are attempting to do—you can listen to what Lady Augusta has to say out of nothing more than gentlemanly behavior if that is all you have within you."

She narrowed her eyes, gesturing towards Augusta with one hand. "Lady Augusta could easily have kept what she has overheard to herself, could have left you to deal with such matters alone, could have laughed as your reputation became clouded, watching the rumors and the gossip surround you. But instead, she has written to you on three occasions and, not satisfied that you had read what she had written and were fully aware of what might occur this evening, has then sought you out so that you might hear it from her lips. And you stand there, in your arrogance, and speak such callous, cruel words that your only purpose, I am sure, is to injure Lady Augusta in any way you can."

Lady Mary said nothing more but turned back towards Augusta, looking angrier than Augusta had ever seen her. "Come, Lady Augusta," she said as Augusta caught the admiration in Lord Dryden's eyes as he watched Lady Mary depart. "Let us leave Lord Leicestershire to himself. He does not want to hear you speak, and I shall not permit him to treat you with such intolerance and malice."

Augusta hesitated, looking at Lord Leicestershire, who was white-faced, his eyes huge as he stared after Lady Mary as if he could not quite believe that she had spoken to him with such authority. Part of her wanted to remain, to tell him exactly what she had overheard, whilst the other begged her to turn away with Lady Mary and allow the consequences of what she had heard to fall upon his head. After all, she told herself, it was something that he deserved.

"This will only be the first," she said, surprised at how tired and weak her voice sounded. "I am sure that more is intended for you, Lord Leicestershire." She bobbed a curtsy, knowing that, even if she had been asked to say more, there was no time left for her to do so. "I do hope you have an enjoyable evening."

Walking from the box with Lady Mary by her side, Augusta felt her spirits lift just a little. "I did not know you had such fire within you, Lady Mary," she said softly, glancing down at her friend and seeing the fierce anger still burning within her gaze. "You were quite furious!"

"As you ought to be also," Lady Mary retorted with a sharp shake of her head. "Lord Leicestershire had no reason to speak to you with such callousness, ought not to have brought you any shame when all you were doing— when all you have done—is an attempt to warn him from whatever it is that is lying in wait for him after this evening."

"At the interval," Augusta murmured, half to herself and half to Lady Mary. "I do not know what these ladies plan to do, nor what the outcome they hope for will be, but I am quite sure that Lord Leicestershire will be all the worse for it."

Lady Mary sniffed and shot a hard glance towards Augusta. "And it shall be his own doing," she said smartly, with such force that Augusta knew she could not argue with her. "He refused to listen, refused even to *read* the notes that you had so kindly written to him, and thus, whatever now occurs is entirely on his head. You cannot take any responsibility, Lady Augusta. You have done your best and that is all that is required."

Augusta considered this, then sighed, shook her head, and dropped her shoulders. "It does not feel as though I have done all I ought," she said, her features twisting in confusion. "I feel as though I ought to go back to Lord Leicestershire, demand that he sit down and then tell him everything that happened without interruption." She chuckled, wondering if Lord Leicestershire would ever allow her to have such an audience with him and knowing full well that he most likely would not. "But it is as you say. I have attempted to inform him, have even attempted to speak to him, and he does not wish to hear it from me."

Lady Mary sighed and put her hand through Augusta's arm, her anger now fading. "I do hope his words did not bring about too much pain," she said quietly as Augusta shook her head. "I know he spoke with great harshness, and even I felt the sting."

"I will not pretend that they did not hurt," Augusta admitted as they walked into the box. "But thanks to your great willingness to stand up for me, to tell Lord Leicestershire such truths without apparently any qualms, I feel emboldened and encouraged once more."

Smiling at her friend, they walked into the box together, only to each receive a scolding from their respective mothers for disappearing without informing them as to where they were going and for *almost* being tardy in their return. Augusta bore this with good grace, apologizing quietly and knowing that she could never tell her mother such things, could never explain what had happened. Sitting down in her seat, she exchanged a quick glance with Lady Mary, smiling lightly, before finally the curtain rose and the play began.

～

"You ARE BEING mysterious this evening, Lady Augusta."

Augusta said nothing in reply, looking at Lady Newfield and finding herself struggling to find an answer.

"Is there something wrong?" Lady Newfield asked gently, looking up into Augusta's face. "You snuck away with Lady Mary before the play began and now it seems as though you wish to hurry away again." Sharp eyes looked into Augusta's, needling her to speak the truth even though she knew she ought to remain silent. She did not know what it was about Lady Newfield, but there was something about her presence that almost forced Augusta to tell her everything.

"I fear Lord Leicestershire is in some danger," she stammered, not quite certain why she had spoken the truth and yet feeling glad about it. "I have tried to speak to him, but he will not listen."

Lady Newfield's face lit up. "I see," she said as though she were delighted by this news. "And you, being his betrothed, are upset that he will not listen to what you have to say?"

Augusta nodded, catching sight of Lady Mary

standing a few paces behind Lady Newfield, desperation flickering in her eyes. "Pray, might I ask you to keep what you have noticed from my mother?" Heat captured her cheeks, but she forced herself to continue speaking. "I do not want her to be upset."

Lady Newfield nodded slowly, no smile on her face but rather a sense of understanding. "But of course," she said slowly. "Although might I give you a little advice, Lady Augusta?" The wisdom that was in her eyes had Augusta nodding profusely, waiting eagerly now to hear what the lady had to say.

Lady Newfield smiled softly. "There are times when a gentleman might need to fall in order to realize what he ought to have done," she told Augusta carefully. "If he will not listen when you have tried to speak to him, then that is his own doing. And mayhap that will be precisely what he needs."

Augusta swallowed hard, aware she felt a flicker of guilt in her heart that she had not been able to force Lord Leicestershire to listen to her.

"Do not feel any guilt over this," Lady Newfield continued, pressing Augusta's hand as though she knew precisely what she had been thinking. "Do what you must but do not cling onto any sort of guilt. It is not yours to take." And with that, Lady Newfield turned on her heel and made her way through the crowd of guests, allowing Lady Mary to hurry forward.

"We must hurry!" Lady Mary whispered, grasping Augusta's hand and beginning to tug her forward, practically rushing her through the crowd that had formed as the many, many guests left their boxes and sought both refreshment and company so that idle chatter about the play itself as well as any new pieces of gossip might be shared between them. Many of those who attended the theatres did not come to see the play or performance, but rather to ensure that they watched those about them. On more than one occasion, Augusta had caught sight of the glint and gleam of theatre eyeglasses as they swept across the theatre, with the lady behind them clearly searching for something that was either of noteworthy interest or something she could share as gossip later.

Her heart was beating quickly as she scanned the crowd for any sign of Lord Leicestershire. She could not see him anywhere, her stomach tightening as Lady Mary continued to pull her through the crowd. The words of Lady Newfield burned in her mind, forcing her to realize that she had nothing to fear for herself. She *had* done what had been required, and Lord Leicestershire, should anything happen, would have no one to blame but himself.

"I do not think he is here," she said, only for Lady Mary to come to a sudden stop, her eyes widening as she looked to her right, her head turned in one direction. Augusta came to a standstill, seeing Lord Leicestershire speaking in a very jovial fashion to a gentleman she did not know.

"Mayhap I was wrong," she said softly, half to herself. "Mayhap I have been quite foolish and—"

"Look!"

As Augusta watched, she saw Lady Whitaker begin to approach him. Her brows lowered as a ripple of distaste ran over her skin. She did not much care for Lady

Whitaker, although she and her mother had, of course, attended the afternoon tea so as not to offend the lady. Lady Whitaker was rich and titled but did not seem to care that she was wed. She flirted with the gentlemen of the *ton* as though she were nothing more than a young debutante, eager to catch the eye of anyone who cared to glance her way.

It appeared she was behaving so now, for Lord Leicestershire was the sole beneficiary of her attention. She put a hand on his arm and laughed loudly at something he said, seeming to suggest that his remark was quite delightful. Augusta turned her gaze away, feeling a sickening sensation in her stomach as she saw just how eagerly Lord Leicestershire seemed to accept Lady Whitaker's attention. It was as though he reveled in it, laughing along with her, his eyes bright and a smile on his face—a smile that he had never once bestowed upon her.

"I do not think there is any need to stand and stare," she said to Lady Mary, dully. "Come now. I am sure that I have made a mistake and there is nothing here for us to watch."

Lady Mary shook her head, biting her lip. "I think you are quite mistaken," she said firmly. "Come now, Lady Augusta, if you are to be proven correct, if Lord Leicestershire is to be made aware of his folly, then we must simply stand and wait."

Augusta shook her head. There was something within her that was almost painful, burning her skin at the thought of having to watch Lord Leicestershire endure some humiliation, even if it *was* his own doing.

"Lady Whitaker is departing," Lady Mary breathed,

forcing Augusta to use almost all her strength to prevent herself from turning her head again to look. "Mayhap we have been mistaken." She frowned, glancing up at Augusta for a moment. "The interval is soon to end and we—"

Her face paled, her hand tightening on Augusta's as she stared at Lord Leicestershire. Augusta, unable to prevent herself any longer, turned to look, only to see Lord Leicestershire following after Lady Whitaker.

Her burning pain heightened, and she closed her eyes, turning her whole body away from him. "I want to return to the box now, Lady Mary," she told her friend. "I have tried to warn him of the dangers that come with being within society, of being so much the source of attention, but he will not listen. And now, it seems, he is to go headlong into it and I, for one, do not want to witness it, not if he is walking into it eagerly."

Lady Mary nodded sympathetically, her eyes huge with evident surprise. "I did not think he would be so overt," she muttered as Augusta winced. "Perhaps he is a little more—oh!"

A muffled scream caught the attention of everyone, including Augusta and Lady Mary. Together, they turned to see the crowd stepping forward as one to where the sound had come from and found themselves moving with them.

"I must apologize!" Lord Leicestershire's voice was loud and filled with regret, though Augusta could not see him as yet. "I did not mean to—"

"My gown!" cried another voice as Augusta finally managed to see the source of consternation. A young lady was propping herself up with one hand, attempting to rise from where she had fallen. Someone came to her aid and helped her to her feet, leaving the young lady looking down at her cream gown, which now had a dull red stain running from her chest to the very bottom. Lord Leicestershire had scrambled up, an empty wine glass by his feet, clearly quite horrified with what had occurred.

"You were attempting to steal my daughter away!" cried another voice, which led to a ripple of astonishment rushing over the gathered crowd. "Did she refuse you? And thus, you did *this* to her?"

Lord Leicestershire began to gesticulate. "I did no such thing!" he exclaimed, his face beginning to redden as he saw the way that all of the *ton* now watched him. "I tripped, that is all. I did not mean to fall into your daughter—a lady I am not even acquainted with—and certainly had no intention of—"

"My gown is quite ruined!" the young lady wailed, her fair head turning this way and that as though to ensure that everyone present could see what she spoke of. "How can I bear such disgrace?"

"I will pay for a new gown, of course," Lord Leicestershire said at once as the crowd began to murmur amongst themselves with excited whispers, telling Augusta that there were those amongst them who thought this to be quite wonderful, for it would give them fresh gossip to chew over for the next few weeks. "And for another one also, so as to make up for any embarrassment I have caused you."

An older lady, who thus far had been hidden by the presence of the young lady, stepped forward, her eyes sharp and narrowed. She pressed one finger up to Lord Leicestershire's chest, her chin lifted and her jaw set.

"And you shall stay away from my daughter," she said, her voice hoarse yet seeming to fill the room. "I know what your brother was, Lord Leicestershire, and there is nothing yet to convince me that you are in any way different from him."

Augusta swallowed hard, seeing the color drain from Lord Leicestershire's face and feeling the urge deep within her to go to him, to support him in his difficulty. With an effort, she set such a desire aside, turning her head away so that she would not see him struggle any longer. Why she had such feelings, she could not say, especially when he had been so quick to disregard her, when he had made it quite clear that he wanted to put an end to the agreement between their families. And yet, it lingered there, to the point that Augusta had to take Lady Mary's arm, using her as an anchor to ensure that she remained steadfast.

"I am not the same gentleman as my brother, I assure you." Lord Leicestershire's voice was strong, but there was a hint of desperation in his expression that Augusta did not miss. When he lifted his head to say the same thing again to the gathered crowd, she saw him catch her eye. He was silent for a moment, his jaw working, battling with a swell of emotion that she did not fully understand.

"I am not my brother," he said again, but Augusta had heard and seen enough. With a heavy heart, she turned away, with Lady Mary still by her side, making to return to her box. There was no need for her to remain any longer. She had tried to warn him, and it had fallen on deaf ears. The consequences were now for him alone to bear and she did not need to feel even a twinge of guilt.

"Let us hope that he might come to see society for what it is," she murmured without even a faint flicker of hope that Lord Leicestershire would do anything other than continue as he was, leaving her behind in his shadow, watching from a distance and battling her strange, perplexing feelings that left her so confused. There was nothing else for her to do.

CHAPTER SEVEN

I t was more than a little apparent that society had
turned a little against him. Stephen shook his head as
he wandered along the street, not quite certain where he
was to go nor what he was to do, but finding the thought
of returning to his townhouse to sit alone as he had done
the last two days to be more than a little depressing.
What made it all the worse was that he had discovered
his signet ring had disappeared from his hand. It had
always been a little large for his finger, but he had worn it
steadfastly, aware of his right and requirement to do so.
For it to be gone now made his heart ache all the more,
fearful that he was not fit to hold the title.

Had he lost it last evening when he had managed to
make such a fool of himself? He could not quite recall
what had happened. The events seemed to be a little
blurry, for one moment he had been following after Lady
Whitaker, only to find himself practically catapulted into
another young lady who had seemingly stepped out of
nowhere. Over and over, he replayed it in his mind, the

details still fuzzy. Had she been pushed? Had she deliberately fallen into him? Either way, he had managed to throw his glass of wine all over the young lady and thereafter, her mother had practically accused him of trying to seduce her daughter when he had no knowledge of her name, her title, and had never once even seen her face before!

Closing his eyes for a moment, Stephen took a deep breath and set his shoulders. Many young ladies had looked at each other as they had walked past him, appearing to be a little wary now rather than eager to be in his company as they had been before. Having had very little to do with society before now, Stephen was astonished to find just how quickly the *ton* had now changed their view of him. They no longer pressed forward, eager to know him, but rather watched him with a good measure of caution, uncertain as to how he might act.

And all because of some foolish mistake.

"Good afternoon, Lord Leicestershire."

Stephen stopped dead as Lady Whitaker bobbed a quick curtsy, her eyes warm but no smile on her face. "Good afternoon," he said tersely, not certain what to make of the lady.

Lady Whitaker tilted her head. "It was an unfortunate situation that overtook you, Lord Leicestershire."

"One I hope you had nothing whatsoever to do with," Stephen said before he could halt his foolish tongue. Seeing the shock ripple across Lady Whitaker's face, he dropped his head and let out a long sigh, heat climbing up his spine. "Forgive me, Lady Whitaker. I spoke without consideration."

"Yes, you did," she said firmly, her eyes no longer holding any warmth whatsoever. "I had nothing to do with poor Miss Hartnett, I can assure you."

"I am sorry," he said heavily, rubbing one hand over his eyes. "I should not have spoken so. I can assure you, I do not place any blame on your shoulders, Lady Whitaker." Sighing, he shook his head, biting his lip. "I do not know how to remove this supposed guilt from my shoulders. It seems as though the *beau monde* now consider me to be just as much a rake as my brother."

Lady Whitaker considered this for a moment, then shrugged. "I am sure that you will be able to step out from it very soon," she said without giving any indication of when she thought such a thing might happen. "Gossip tends to run from one thing to the next. Within the sennight, you will no longer be the topic of discussion on so many a person's lips."

This did not bring any relief to Stephen's heart, for a sennight felt very long indeed and he did not want to let himself consider what would occur within that time. He had just become used to the attention showered on him by society, had enjoyed the way that so many people were eager for his attention—and now they turned away from him, their eyes holding suspicion and doubt.

"I can help you, of course," Lady Whitaker continued, speaking with great slowness as though she were considering every word. "That is, if you would *wish* for my assistance, Lord Leicestershire?"

He began to nod, only to stop himself, seeing the way her brows lifted in expectation of delight, feeling that same swirling in his stomach that had come last evening when he had first realized what had happened. Lady Whitaker was offering him something, but he was not certain what it was.

"I think I shall simply suffer for the sennight," he told her, seeing the way her brows lowered almost at once, a line between them now and a thinness to her lips that had not been there before. "I shall prove to the *ton* that I am not a rogue. I shall behave impeccably and speak to everyone with great politeness in the hope that they will be convinced by that."

Lady Whitaker lifted her chin, a dark glint to her eyes that had not been there before. "You are not enamoring yourself with me, Lord Leicestershire," she told him, making him wince inwardly. "I am offering to do what I can for you. Do you not understand?" She took a small step closer to him, and Stephen immediately felt the urge to move away but forced himself not to do so. "I am a wealthy lady with wonderful connections and all of society practically at my feet." She smiled at him, but her gaze remained hard. "If you came to stand by my side, if we were seen out and about in society together, then within the week, the *ton* would know that they were mistaken in their worries about you."

Stephen swallowed hard, finding it more and more difficult to extricate himself. The last thing he wanted was to make the situation worse and, whilst he did not know Lady Whitaker particularly well, he was a little fearful that drawing close to her, as she suggested, was quite the wrong thing to do. Clearing his throat, he happened to glance around him only to see none other than Lady Augusta and Lady Mary walking together, their smiles and bright eyes quite at odds with how he felt. Without intending to do so, Stephen found his eyes lingering on Lady Augusta until, perhaps feeling his intense look, she turned her head and caught his gaze.

"Lord Leicestershire?"

Giving himself a slight shake, Stephen looked back to Lady Whitaker, seeing her expectant expression and berating himself inwardly for not finding a decent excuse with which he might extricate himself.

"Lady Whitaker," he said carefully, wondering how he would express his disinclination without upsetting her. "I think that I—"

"Lord Leicestershire, good afternoon!" Lady Augusta had come towards them both in only a matter of moments, saving him from his awkward situation. "And Lady Whitaker, how very good to see you again." She smiled warmly at Lady Whitaker, who struggled to rearrange her features from disappointment and frustration at being so interrupted, to happiness at being met by two acquaintances.

"Good afternoon," she murmured as Lady Mary smiled at them both. "Are you out together this afternoon? Mayhap you have thought to find a new ribbon?" There was a touch of hopefulness in Lady Whitaker's voice, and Stephen turned his eyes directly towards Lady Augusta, silently trying to convey his eagerness that she would not hurry away. Lady Augusta glanced at him, but her expression did not change. Instead, she kept smiling at Lady Whitaker and told her that she and Lady Mary had decided to take a short stroll through town.

"My mother is with us also," Lady Mary continued,

glancing over her shoulder. "But she continues to find people to converse with, and so we have not made a good deal of progress this afternoon!"

Lady Whitaker smiled and murmured something that Stephen could not quite make out, with Lady Mary throwing him a quick glance also.

"I am certain she would be very glad to speak to you," Lady Mary said, stepping to one side and extending her arm towards her mother, who was now standing a short distance away, talking animatedly to another lady, whom Stephen did not recognize. "Please, Lady Whitaker, do join me."

Stephen held his breath as Lady Whitaker glanced at him, giving her what he hoped was a rueful look, which, thankfully, she accepted without question. Excusing herself quietly, she walked towards Lady Mary and together, they walked away from Stephen and Lady Augusta.

There came a silence between them that had Stephen clearing his throat and dropping his gaze. He did not know what to say. He had been brusque in his manner towards Lady Augusta, had spoken disparagingly to her when she had been attempting to help him. Had he listened to her, had he been able to overcome his foolish pride, then he might have avoided the disastrous situation with Miss Hartnett.

"I—I should have listened to you, Lady Augusta."

The words came out in a rush, his tongue tripping over his teeth as he attempted to overcome the embarrassment that came with speaking so openly.

"I believe that what happened with Miss Hartnett

was, somehow, arranged by whomever it was that you overheard speaking in the bookshop," he continued quickly. "I was foolish in my eagerness to disregard what you said. It was very kind of you—very *considerate* of you—to come in search of me, particularly after what I have told you I intend to do." He had not done a good deal in that regard, he realized, aside from telling his solicitors that he wished for them to find a way to remove him from his betrothal agreement. "I fear I have misjudged you, Lady Augusta. Your advice to me, your words of truth—whilst difficult to accept at times—have all been quite correct."

Lady Augusta let out a slow breath as though she was not quite certain whether or not to believe him. Her eyes were dark green pools, her lips firm as they pressed together, considering.

"I do not know nor understand society," Stephen muttered, closing his eyes and turning his head away with the shame of it. "I have spent so many years on the outskirts, seeing how the *beau monde* sought out my brother, how the young ladies chased after him, and how they were so eager to make his acquaintance, always telling myself that it was all quite foolish and false. And now, since I have taken on my brother's title, I have found myself in a situation that I have never once been in before." He shrugged as though such a remark would make sense. "I have been eager to pursue it, I suppose. I have enjoyed the attention. And yet, you warned me that there was a darkness within society, but I did not see it. I *chose* not to see it."

Lady Augusta's expression softened. "I believe you

were trying to avoid giving an answer of some description to Lady Whitaker," she said, a question within her statement. "I have tried to tell you before now, Lord Leicestershire, to be careful when it comes to your acquaintance with the lady. Mayhap now, you will be able to understand my reason for such a warning."

He nodded. "I was, in fact, attempting to extricate myself from her very kind offer of accompanying me throughout society so that I might be able to overcome this very strange situation I now find myself in. A situation where I have lost something of the standing I was once in, as well as the signet ring that was upon my finger. I fear as though I am not meant to be within society, Lady Augusta, that I have failed in the most dreadful of ways."

"You fear that you are now viewed with suspicion rather than outright happiness at your company," Lady Augusta replied with a knowing look. "Might I ask what you said to Lady Whitaker?"

Stephen allowed himself a small smile. "I was trying to find a way to refuse her offer," he told Lady Augusta, looking over to where Lady Mary and Lady Whitaker were now talking together. "As much as I would like to return to the status I had only a short time ago, I fear that it will merely take time for the *ton* to believe that I am *not* the rogue they think me to be."

Lady Augusta turned her head, following his gaze. "That is wise, Lord Leicestershire." Looking back at him, she twisted her lips to one side, still considering him. "I would offer to take up Lady Whitaker's offer in her place, but I fear that you would not accept me."

Stephen was staggered. It was as though the last few days had not occurred at all as though everything they knew about each other had evaporated entirely. How could she be so willing to come and assist him now, when he had been so cruel towards her?

"You need not accept," Lady Augusta continued, after only a momentary hesitation. "I can see that you have—"

"Please, please." Stephen waved his hand in front of his face, giving himself a slight shake to regain himself a little. "It is not that I want to refuse, Lady Augusta, but rather that I find myself so confused by your generosity and kind spirit that I feel myself both ashamed and thoroughly unworthy of your willingness."

Lady Augusta did not blush and look away, did not smile sweetly nor shake her head as though to push his words away, but instead, she simply continued to watch him, her eyes searching his face and finding some answer to whatever questions were going about her mind. She sighed and her shoulders dropped, relaxing just a little.

"Lord Leicestershire, I made a very poor first impression," she said, spreading her hands out to either side. "I was less than willing to be your bride. I was upset that my father had made this arrangement without even considering me. It had all come as a great shock and I did not treat you as I should have." She shook her head, her smile rueful. "And thereafter, when you returned to society after your mourning, I found myself upset as to how changed you appeared. I know that I only met you for a short time, but I was aware of your quiet reserve, how you kept yourself back from society. I watched you for some time before we were introduced, Lord Leicestershire, and saw that what I had been told of you was quite true." One shoulder lifted. "Then to see you so eager to throw yourself headlong into society, to accept their attention when their eagerness to know you is simply because they want to take what they can from you, rather irritated me. Again, I did not behave well. I was foolish and sought to be spiteful in retaliation."

Her eyes held his, her cheeks coloring but her gaze steady. "I will not pretend that your decision to seek an end to our betrothal has not brought me distress, but neither will I allow it to influence how we now converse and behave towards each other. I can understand your decision since you are now a marquess and thus have much more to consider regarding your future." Her shoulder dropped. "Might we consider ourselves acquaintances, Lord Leicestershire?" she asked, a slight lift to her voice, clearly hoping that he would be willing to set the past aside. "I would be glad to come alongside you, Lord Leicestershire, to prove to society that you are not the rogue that your brother once was and," she finished, glancing away, looking a little abashed, "perhaps the opportunity to discover who was speaking at the bookshop that day, and why they are so inclined towards bringing you such shame and embarrassment."

It was a very great speech, and as she finished, Lady Augusta let out a long breath as though she had said all she wished and was now quite relieved with it all. Stephen found that his throat was a little sore, as though his whole being was struggling to find a suitable response.

"I think I do not know you at all, Lady Augusta," he

managed to say, his voice wavering just a little with the swell of emotion in his chest. "I have misjudged you. I have shown you no consideration. I have been cruel and unkind—deliberately so—and did not even think of listening to you when I ought to have done so."

To his surprise, Lady Augusta stepped forward, her hand on his arm for just a moment, her eyes crinkled at the corners as she smiled.

"Might we say, Lord Leicestershire, that we have both made mistakes and errors in judgment?" she said softly, her hand dropping back to her side. "Will that satisfy you? There is no need for either of us to torment our hearts with guilt and regret."

A sense of sheer relief pressed into his soul, and he nodded fervently, hardly able to lift his eyes from her. "I would be most grateful for such a kindness, Lady Augusta," he said quietly. "I thank you. And, yes, I would be just as glad for your presence, at any time you would wish to give it."

She smiled at him, and he felt his heart twist in his chest, feeling as though he were seeing her for the very first time. He had made so many mistakes, but apparently, Lady Augusta was more than willing to forget about them in the hope that he would do the same for her.

"And without speaking ill of Lady Whitaker, I would be very careful in your acquaintance with her," Lady Augusta said, her voice dropping so that there would be no chance of Lady Whitaker hearing her. "There are rumors about her friendship with certain gentlemen here in London, all whilst her husband remains at his estate."

"I see," Stephen muttered, aware of the flush that crept into his cheeks.

"Might I ask why you were following after her at the theatre, on the night you fell into Miss Hartnett?"

"Following Lady Whitaker?" Stephen asked, seeing Lady Augusta frown and aware now of her concern regarding the lady. "It was nothing of importance. It was only that Lady Whitaker thought to introduce me to a gentleman of her acquaintance—a Lord Garretson, if I recall correctly—and she was merely seeking him out." He shrugged. "When she beckoned to me, I followed after her, only to...to fall into Miss Harnett."

Lady Augusta nodded slowly, her brow furrowed. "I did not see precisely what happened," she said. "But I have spoken to Lady Whitaker on many previous occasions, and I am quite certain that it was not her voice that I heard on the day I was in the bookshop."

He nodded, finding himself now quite eager to discover who had done such a thing to him and their reasons behind it. "That is not to say that she could not have come to the aid of someone else."

Lady Augusta smiled. "That is true, of course," she agreed. "But for the moment, let us try to encourage society back towards you and, mayhap from that, we will discover something of importance."

He inclined his head, feeling such a sense of happiness that he could not help but extend his hand to her. When she gave it to him, he bowed over it, his lips only an inch or so from her skin. The urge to press his mouth to it overcame him, and he found himself doing precisely that, even though he knew that such a thing was showing a strong regard for the lady. A regard that he hoped she understood was a deep sense of gratitude for what she had offered him.

"We—we should return to Lady Mary." Lady Augusta pulled her hand back again, practically snatching it from him before turning on her heel and making her way towards her friend, leaving him to follow after. A little embarrassed, Stephen cleared his throat, put his hands behind his back, and fell into step behind her. Within a few minutes, he had greeted the rest of the ladies and had heard of their plans to take a turn about St. James' Park once they had enjoyed a short respite at Gunter's, where they hoped to enjoy an ice.

"Might you wish to join us, Lord Leicestershire?" Lady Augusta asked, her smile bright and a slight gleam in her eye that told him that she truly did want him to attend. "It is a very fine day, indeed."

"I would be very glad to do so," he told her, seeing how she smiled and feeling his heart lift. "So long as none of the others regret having me within their company, given what some might think of my presence."

Lady Mary shook her head vehemently, even though it took Lady Mary's mother a few moments to agree with her daughter. Lady Whitaker, who seemed to think that his agreement meant that he wanted to spend a little more time in her company, pressed his arm for a moment, evidently meant in reassurance but only served to send an unwelcome shiver up his spine.

"Then shall we make our way to Gunter's?" Lady Augusta asked, and the group turned as one and began to meander along the pavement, each talking to the other.

Stephen followed behind Lady Augusta, taking her in and finding himself feeling much happier than he had been when he had first stepped into town. He felt almost protected by their company, as though they were willing to save him from the whispers that would chase after him the moment he stepped into St. James' Park. Lifting his head a little higher, he felt his courage grow and his determination build. Together with Lady Augusta, he would make certain to prove to the *ton* that all that had occurred had been a mere mistake and not an indication of the sort of gentleman he was. They would come to think well of him again; he was quite certain. All it would take was a little time—and Lady Augusta's company.

CHAPTER EIGHT

"I have heard you have been seen spending a little more time with Lord Leicestershire, Augusta."

Augusta swallowed hard and looked up at her father, who was sitting opposite her at the breakfast table, his voice a little muffled as he spoke to her from behind his newspapers. The truth was, whilst she had been seen in Lord Leicestershire's company, all of society had been speaking about him in most unfavorable terms the last few days. Yesterday afternoon, they had walked in St. James' Park, and she had been very aware of the sidelong glances that had been sent her way, as well as the hard looks that came from one or two gentlemen. Most likely, this had been what her father had heard of, although given he was speaking to her from behind his newspaper, she could not gauge his reaction.

"Yes, Father," she said, suddenly wondering if Lord Leicestershire had spoken with her father and had made it clear that he wanted to bring an end to the arrangement between them. "I do hope that is not displeasing to you."

The papers shuffled slightly. "I have heard of the incident that occurred at the theatre," Lord Elmsworth said, clearing his throat. "I must confess, I do not know what to make of it."

"I think it nothing more than an unfortunate accident," Augusta replied firmly as the newspapers were lowered, and her father's heavy-lidded eyes looked back at her steadily. "I believe his word when he says that he had no intention of knocking into Miss Hartnett."

Lord Elmsworth nodded slowly, his brows still furrowed. "His brother was a rake and a rascal," he said, uneasily. "I was assured, in our discussions, that he was nothing akin to his brother."

"I am certain he is just as he seems," Augusta replied with a smile that felt a little unsteady. "I hope that you will continue to trust him, Father. As I am doing." She did not mention anything of what had passed between herself and Lord Leicestershire, did not speak to him about the awkwardness that still lingered between them. She held her father's gaze and felt her stomach tighten. Had Lord Leicestershire spoken to Lord Elmsworth and expressed his desire to be free of the engagement? "Do you wish me to remove myself from his company?"

Lord Elmsworth considered this for a few moments, his eyes roving across the room as he thought. Augusta held her breath, her hands in her lap and her fingers twisting together as she looked at her father.

"No," Lord Elmsworth said eventually, nodding to himself as though he had only just made a decision and was now quite satisfied with it. "I think that you ought to continue as you are, Augusta. However," he cleared his throat and looked at her sharply. "If there is any other untoward behavior from him, if there is any sort of roguish nonsense that brings both him and you disgrace and upset, then you must tell me at once."

Augusta let out her breath slowly, not wanting to show any sort of relief on her face but rather keeping her expression fairly impassive. "Of course, Father."

"A man can be greatly altered by a change in his circumstances," Lord Elmsworth commented, lifting his newspapers back up in front of his face again, bringing an end to their conversation. "As much as I think this arrangement would be a most excellent match, I do not want you to be in any way mistreated, Augusta."

"I thank you, Father," she murmured, rising from her chair and feeling a mixture of relief and happiness swirling through her as she made her way to the door. Lord Leicestershire, it seemed, had not yet managed to find a way to remove himself from their betrothal agreement and that, for whatever reason, brought her a gladness to her heart. Walking from the room, she felt a lightness about her steps now, her heart lifting within her as she recalled how he had smiled at her yesterday afternoon, how there had been a warmth in his eyes that had filled her heart completely.

Perhaps there was still a chance that their betrothal would continue, that Lord Leicestershire would not seek to bring an end to it all. Now that they had begun their acquaintance anew, Augusta felt a flicker of hope, although she did nothing to encourage it. Rather, she accepted it for what it was and turned her thoughts to what she would be doing next, and to what she would next be doing with Lord Leicestershire.

~

"Good evening, Lady Augusta. Might I hope that you have a dance saved for me?"

Augusta turned around and allowed herself to smile, feeling a kick of nervousness in her heart as she smiled at Lord Leicestershire. "Good evening, Lord Leicestershire," she said, pulling her dance card from her wrist. "I have not yet had a single gentleman sign my dance card. You are more than welcome to choose whatever dances you wish."

Lord Leicestershire inclined his head, although there was no smile on his face as he lifted his eyes to hers. "I fear that you may find other gentlemen less willing to dance with you should they spy my name there," he said, not reaching for her card as she held it out. "Mayhap I should approach you later."

Shaking her head, Augusta pressed the card to him. "Please, Lord Leicestershire," she said encouragingly. "We are attempting to encourage society to see you as you truly are, are we not? Therefore, you must not shy away."

He hesitated still, then with a small nod took her card from her and wrote his name quickly down on not one but two spaces. "I have been bold," he told her, his smile strained. "I do hope this does not impact you poorly, Lady Augusta."

"I am certain it will not," she said, smiling. "And you

must ensure that you find other young ladies to dance with also. Even if you fear they are inclined to refuse you."

He looked away again, a sigh escaping from his mouth. "I understand," he said quietly. "I confess that I am a little afraid that the ladies who attempted—and succeeded—to bring me such embarrassment before might be present this evening and attempt to do so again."

"Be on your guard," she offered, knowing there was not much else for her to say. "And I will, of course, do what I can."

He held out his hand, and without even thinking of it, she gave him her hand and he bowed over it. Feeling heat rippling up her spine and into her face, she looked away as he lifted his head, a little astonished by the sensations that rushed through her.

"I thank you, Lady Augusta," Lord Leicestershire said, sounding truly grateful. "Again, your kindness and encouragement overwhelm me."

She made to say something more, only to see that another young lady was approaching, her eyes fixed upon Lord Leicestershire. Stepping back, she arched one eyebrow and glanced in her direction before flinging her gaze back towards him, only to see him turn his head also.

"Miss Trevelyan," she heard Lord Leicestershire say as she turned around to walk away. "Good evening."

Smiling to herself, she soon caught the eye of Lady Mary, who had been standing only a short distance away, waiting for her to approach.

"You have secured a dance from Lord Leicestershire, I see," Lady Mary said with a warm smile. "He appears to be doing well with Miss Trevelyan, also, which must be an encouragement to him."

"Yes, indeed," Augusta said as two gentlemen of her acquaintance came towards them, bowing to them both. "Ah, good evening, Lord Stockbridge, Lord Clevedon."

"Good evening."

Within a few minutes, Augusta found that she had more dances filled on her dance card, glad to be able to tell Lord Leicestershire that his name on her card made no particular difference to other gentlemen seeking her company. Satisfied, she found herself eagerly looking forward to her dance with Lord Leicestershire, knowing full well that it would be much improved from the last time they had stepped out together!

"You dance well, Lord Leicestershire."

Augusta smiled up at Lord Leicestershire as they completed their waltz, meaning every word as she complimented him.

"Did you expect me to be a poor dancer?" he asked, looking a little affronted before he smiled at her, his lip a little lopsided as he chuckled, making her laugh. "I will admit, whilst I have not danced very often in society, I do know how to do so."

Augusta made to answer and then caught her breath as he whirled her about the floor for the final few spins before the music began to end. Laughing up into his face, she dropped into a curtsy as he bowed, seeing a lightness in his expression that had not been there before.

"I thank you," he said, lifting himself from his bow. "That was most enjoyable."

"I am glad," she said as he offered her his arm, walking from the floor together. "And have you found the evening particularly difficult?"

He hesitated, the light fading from his eyes as he looked away from her. "It has been interesting," he said, more quietly than before. "Not everyone has been as welcoming as they once were."

"That is to be expected but it will not last for long," she said as enthusiastically as she could. "Now, if you would like, I would suggest that—"

"Lord Leicestershire!"

Before she could continue, another young lady came hurrying towards them, her eyes wide.

"Lord Leicestershire, you were tied to me for the waltz!"

Lord Leicestershire stared at the young lady, his cheeks slowly coloring as he began to stammer. "I—I fear you are mistaken, Miss Sidwell."

"I am not!" Her eyes began to fill with tears as she held out her dance card. "Look, your signature is upon it!"

She held out her dance card with a trembling hand, and Lord Leicestershire took it, his eyes searching the card until, finally, Augusta saw his eyes widen.

Her stomach dropped.

"I am—I am terribly sorry," Lord Leicestershire breathed, his words stammering out of him as he tried to find some excuse. "I did not know—"

"You must forgive me."

Augusta saw two pairs of eyes turning towards her, her cheeks heating as she tried to shoulder the blame, to take on the consequences of what Lord Leicestershire had *apparently* done. She did not believe that he had done anything of the sort, of course, feeling quite certain that this was yet another way to undermine Lord Leicestershire by whomever it was that wanted to bring shame to him and damage his reputation.

"I think I have made a mistake," she continued as Miss Sidwell blinked rapidly, her eyes glassy. "I thought it was Lord Leicestershire on my dance card, but now that I have looked at it again..." She lifted it towards herself but did not show it to Miss Sidwell herself. "I think that it is Lord Larchstone that is written there."

Lord Leicestershire stared at her, his jaw working for a moment or two. Miss Sidwell sucked in a breath, still appearing distraught but also, Augusta noticed, looking a little less certain now. Her eyes narrowed as she looked steadily back at Miss Sidwell, noting how the girl dropped her gaze almost at once. What had been said to her to convince her of doing such a thing?

"Lord Leicestershire, I must apologize for convincing you that this particular dance was for me," she continued when neither of the other two said anything. "You did not have time to check your record, given the fact that I was eagerly waiting to step onto the dance floor." She held out one hand to Miss Sidwell, who, after a moment, reached out to take it. "Miss Sidwell, I beg you not to hold Lord Leicestershire accountable. It was entirely my doing and I must beg your forgiveness."

Miss Sidwell said nothing for some moments,

although Augusta squeezed her hand and smiled brightly. She did not seem to know what to say, leaving such a prolonged silence growing between them that there was a sense of awkwardness that now washed over them all.

"You are very gracious, Lady Augusta," Lord Leicestershire said, inclining his head, his eyes holding more thankfulness than he could express at that moment. "I would not like you to take all of the blame, however, for I—"

"Mayhap Miss Sidwell could accept the second dance I have with you, Lord Leicestershire, in the place of what I have taken from her," Augusta said before he could say any more. "I would be more than happy for you to have it, Miss Sidwell, even though it is not the waltz." She smiled brightly at the lady again, but Miss Sidwell only frowned. She seemed to be very unsure of herself now, as though something had disconcerted her.

Lord Leicestershire cleared his throat, inclined his head, and turned towards Miss Sidwell. "Will you forgive me, Miss Sidwell?" he asked, graciously. "And would you accept Lady Augusta's *kind* offer in place of what was meant to be our dance?"

Miss Sidwell glanced to her left, alerting Augusta almost immediately. She wanted desperately to look in the same direction in the hope of seeing whoever it was that had set up this situation, but she knew she could not. Keeping her gaze fixed on the lady, Augusta waited with growing anticipation, beginning to hope that Miss Sidwell might lead them to those who had arranged this— only for Miss Sidwell to sigh heavily and incline her head. Lord Leicestershire beamed at the lady, thanking her profusely and promising to come and seek her out well before their dance was due to begin. Augusta smiled warmly and inclined her head only for Miss Sidwell to excuse herself. To Augusta's surprise, she did not go to her left as Augusta had expected, but rather turned on her heel and began to move through the crowd behind her.

"I should follow her at once," Augusta murmured as Lord Leicestershire let out a heavy breath. "I will be discreet, I promise you."

"Thank you, Lady Augusta."

The relief in Lord Leicestershire's voice stopped her and she turned to him, seeing him running one hand over his eyes and feeling her heart squeeze with sympathy.

"If you had not stepped forward as you did, then I am sure that Miss Sidwell would have made a much greater —and perhaps louder—protest than she did."

"I believe that was the intention," Augusta told him as Lord Leicestershire nodded. "I shall return to your side just as soon as I can, Lord Leicestershire, but for the moment, I must follow her."

Lord Leicestershire nodded, reaching out to press her hand for just a second before she stepped away. Having stopped to listen to Lord Leicestershire, Augusta could no longer see Miss Sidwell, her stomach beginning to flutter with a thousand butterflies as she tried to hurry in the direction she believed Miss Sidwell had gone.

There!

She saw Miss Sidwell still shifting through the crowd, moving slowly and with great care, clearly searching for someone. Her head twisted this way and that, her steps careful. Augusta wondered where Miss Sidwell's guardian or parent was at present, although she herself could not exactly criticize Miss Sidwell for such a thing given she was without her guardian also!

Her brows lowered as Miss Sidwell stopped suddenly, making a small turn to her left and looking straight ahead at whoever was present there. She strained to see, not wanting to go chasing after the lady, but desperately eager to find out who had encouraged Miss Sidwell to behave in such a manner and to claim such a thing as that when Augusta knew for certain that it was nothing more than a lie. Lord Leicestershire's name had been written by another. Miss Sidwell's hurt and upset was entirely feigned with the sole purpose, Augusta was sure, of bringing Lord Leicestershire a public shaming.

"Ah, Lady Augusta!"

A face stepped out of the crowd and stopped directly in front of her, forcing Augusta to look away from Miss Sidwell.

"Lady Villiers," the lady continued, curtsying quickly. "You may not recall me, but I—"

"Yes, yes, of course," Augusta said quickly, trying to let her gaze dart towards Miss Sidwell but finding that she could not do so, could not focus her eyes on where Miss Sidwell stood in the crowd. It would be more than a little rude of her to ignore Lady Villiers, but she simply *had* to see who Miss Sidwell was speaking to.

"I believe we last saw each other at Lady Whitaker's afternoon tea," Lady Villiers said with a tiny gleam in her eye as Augusta's heart filled with frustration. "My daughter introduced us."

"Yes, I recall," Augusta replied quickly, trying to find something to say that would allow herself to be removed from this situation without delay. "You must forgive me, Lady Villiers, I have—"

"And where is your dear friend this evening?" Lady Villiers interrupted as though she had not heard a word of what Augusta had said. "Lady Mary, is it not?"

Battling her irritation and the desire to simply tell Lady Villiers that she was unable to speak openly at present, Augusta let out her breath slowly, forcing a smile to her lips. "Lady Mary is present this evening, yes," she said as Lady Villiers smiled delightedly at this news. "Now, I must beg your pardon, Lady Villiers, but I am in search of my friend and, if I cannot find her, then I must secure my mother's company instead." Putting on what she hoped was an apologetic look, Augusta lifted her shoulders in a small shrug. "I should not be wandering around the ballroom without her company."

Lady Villiers laughed, her eyes twinkling. "I am sure that no one present would condemn you for such a thing, not unless you were to step out of doors," she said with a wide smile. "But you are quite correct, Lady Augusta." With what appeared to be a sense of determination, she turned her head to look about the room. "Come, Lady Augusta, I will ensure that you reach either your friend or your mother without delay. We shall not be prevented!"

Laughing, she began to walk through the crowd, leaving Augusta with no other choice but to follow after her. With a sense of great irritation filling her, she turned her head, trying to see who Miss Sidwell spoke to, but could make nothing out. Frustrated beyond measure, she gritted her teeth and screwed up her hands into fists before, reluctantly, stepping forward away from Miss Sidwell and following after Lady Villiers.

Whoever Miss Sidwell had been speaking to, it was going to have to remain a mystery for the present, leaving Augusta thoroughly exasperated and deeply unsatisfied that she would now have to return to Lord Leicestershire without even the smallest clue and that, Augusta knew, would be deeply disappointing.

"Ah, there is Lady Mary!" A spiral of hope flung itself through Augusta's chest as she saw her friend standing talking to Lord Dryden under the watchful eye of Lady Mary's mother, who was standing a few feet away. "Thank you, Lady Villiers." She bobbed a quick curtsy and made to step away, hoping that she might be able to pull Lady Mary back towards Miss Sidwell again, only for Lady Villiers to let out a trill of laughter and hurry towards Lady Mary.

"I must greet her also, of course!" she exclaimed, flinging her words over her shoulder. "She was also *very* kind to my daughter at Lady Whitaker's afternoon tea and I should be glad to speak to her this evening."

Augusta closed her eyes, her hopes fading to disappointment. "Of course," she muttered, her steps heavy as she followed after her.

It seemed she was to be thwarted once again.

CHAPTER NINE

Whoever had been behind Miss Sidwell's attempt to embarrass and shame him even more at the ball last evening, their intentions were clear. Stephen frowned and rubbed at the lines that had formed on his forehead as he thought, trying to think of who might want to treat him in such a way. The carriage rattled along the London streets, soothing his spirits just a little as he tried to make sense of what had occurred. His thoughts remained blank, his mind struggling to even think of a single soul who would want to shame him, unable to even understand *why* they would do such a thing.

And then, his thoughts turned to Lady Augusta. In a moment, his forehead had cleared, his angst had lifted, and he had found himself smiling. It was astonishing just how much she could lift his spirits, even with just a single thought.

Stephen felt blessed to have been given a second opportunity to know Lady Augusta, finding his heart to be filled with gratitude for her company and her determination to help him through this difficult situation. Society, at least, had not turned their back on him entirely, and yesterday evening had gone as well as expected, but it could have become a good deal worse had Miss Sidwell made a scene over his supposed error. Stephen was quite certain that he had not written his name down on Miss Sidwell's card for the waltz but rather for another dance entirely, but when he had looked at her dance card, he had seen his name written there just as she had said. He had not been certain what she had done or why, but had it not been for Lady Augusta's willingness to step into the fore and take the blame, then he might now have been struggling with society's less-than-considerate view of him.

That being said, he had not been the best of gentlemen last evening. He had struggled to converse and to even pay attention to the ladies he had danced with thereafter. Miss Sidwell had received nothing but the shortest of conversations with him when they had danced, and Miss Trevelyan, Lady Mary, Miss Winchester, and Lady Sophia had found him to be mostly silent. He had received a good many frowns and a few muttered comments from his dance partners and had, on each occasion, apologized profusely for his lack of interest. Miss Trevelyan especially had tried to speak to him and had even mentioned to him that she was not about to turn away from him as some in society had, and all he had been able to do was mutter a few words of gratitude before releasing her to dance with another gentleman, Lord Drake.

Wincing, Stephen looked up out of the carriage

window as it began to slow, turning into Hyde Park for what would be the fashionable hour. He had not wanted to attend, but Lady Augusta had insisted that it would be a wise idea, in order to show the *ton* that he was determined to prove himself to them. However, given last night's attempt to bring him low had been foiled by Lady Augusta, Stephen felt a sense of increased anxiety, worrying that something new might occur that would set him on an even darker path. Taking in a deep breath, he sat up straight and looked steadfastly out of the window, determined to give the appearance of being at ease.

Calling his carriage to halt, he climbed out and made certain his hat was straight. With proud steps, he walked forward into the park, very well aware there were a good many eyes watching his every move.

"Good afternoon, Lord Leicestershire," someone purred, and he glanced to his right to see a lady he did not know coming towards him. His heart began to beat furiously and he was forced to make a decision—either he could remain and speak to this lady, even though he did not believe they had been introduced, or he could ignore her greeting and continue as though he had not heard it.

He chose the latter. Clearing his throat, he turned his head away and continued to walk, ignoring the lady and her greeting completely. As he made his way further into the crowd, he heard the murmurs and laughter of conversation rushing towards him on every side, making his chest tighten. Were they speaking about him? Had he chosen the wrong course of action?

"Good afternoon, Lord Leicestershire."

There came the very same greeting as before, but this

time, it came from none other than Miss Trevelyan, who was standing beside her mother, Lady Villiers. The two young ladies Miss Trevelyan had been speaking to only moments before became entirely silent, their eyes widening as they looked at him in evident astonishment that Miss Trevelyan had spoken to him in such a welcoming tone. Beside them was a gentleman that Stephen vaguely recognized—was it Lord Drake from the previous evening?

"Miss Trevelyan," Stephen murmured, bowing low. "And Lady Villiers. Good afternoon." Lifting his head, he graced them both with as warm a smile as he could, praying that they would not have noticed him ignoring the lady he did not know only a few moments before. "It is a very fine day, is it not?"

"It is made all the better with your company, Lord Leicestershire," Miss Trevelyan said with a gentle lift of one eyebrow which both surprised him and sent a small stab of worry into his chest. "Might I introduce my acquaintances to you?"

Stephen nodded, seeing the glimmer of a smile on Lady Villiers' features and the glint in her eye. The introductions were made, and he greeted both young ladies with a bow, noting how they both glanced at each other before dropping into a quick curtsy. Clearly, there were still a good many whispers about him amongst society.

"And you know Lord Drake, of course."

Stephen nodded to the gentleman, who grinned in an ugly fashion, although Stephen did not much linger upon his expression.

"Might I ask if you had an enjoyable evening last

night, Lord Leicestershire?" Lady Villiers asked as Stephen nodded. "You were dancing with my daughter on two occasions, I believe?"

"Just the once," he corrected her with a tight smile. "I am afraid that I was not the most attentive of gentlemen last evening, Lady Villiers."

"Oh?" Lady Villiers glanced at her daughter, who had pinned her gaze to Stephen's features. "And why might that be, Lord Leicestershire?"

He blinked, not having any intention of explaining himself and a little surprised at Lady Villiers' forwardness. Clearing his throat gruffly, he looked down at the ground for a moment, trying to work out what to say.

"There are...rumors about my character, Lady Villiers, that I am certain you are fully aware of," he said, a little awkwardly. "As such, not everyone is willing to consider my presence beside them."

"Rumors that I am *certain* hold no truth," Miss Trevelyan said warmly, with such certainty in her voice that he looked at her sharply, wondering what it was she was trying to express. "You must be aware, Lord Leicestershire, that there are those of us within the *ton* that give no credence to any such rumors."

"And for that, I am very grateful," he told her, his gaze snagging on something—or rather, someone—who had just stepped down from her carriage. "I..." He had not realized that he had trailed off, for his whole being was, at that moment, entirely fixed to Lady Augusta. She was clad in a light green gown, with a bright smile on her face and a warmth to her expression that seemed to make the sunny day brighten all the more. She appeared to be aware he was watching her, for within only a few moments, she was looking back directly into his eyes and her smile was one that brought a swirl of contentment to his heart.

Why had he ever thought to bring their betrothal to an end?

"You were saying, Lord Leicestershire?"

Starting in surprise, he looked to see Miss Trevelyan's face quite changed. She no longer bore that warmth in her expression but a hardness that brought lines to her forehead and a thinness to her rosebud mouth. "Ah, yes," he stammered, a trifle awkwardly. "I apologize." Bowing to them all, he took a step back, unable to resist the urge that was within his heart to go towards Lady Augusta without hesitation as though he was afraid she might speak to another person and thus leave him to simply stand to watch her. "If you would excuse me, Lady Villiers, I should allow you to continue your conversation with the Miss Johnstones and Lord Drake." With a tight smile at the ladies, he gave a quick bow and then took his leave, hurrying towards Lady Augusta without making any attempt to hide his eagerness.

Lady Augusta looked towards him, perhaps aware, somehow, that he had been intending to seek her out. Her smile sent his heart singing, his happiness seeming to build with every step he took.

"Lord Leicestershire," Lady Augusta said, bobbing a curtsy, her eyes a little demure. "Good afternoon."

"I am *very* glad to see you," he found himself saying,

speaking with such fervency that he surprised himself with his eagerness. "I had not the opportunity to properly thank you last evening for what you did."

Lady Augusta laughed, just as her mother, accompanied by Lady Newfield, came towards him, greeting him with a quick smile and a murmur of welcome. There was a quick introduction to Lady Newfield, who watched them both with a sharp eye, making him wonder if she knew more about him than she expressed. Stephen exchanged pleasantries for a few minutes and then held out his arm to Lady Augusta, hoping that she would accept him.

"Might I walk with you for a few minutes, Lady Augusta?" he asked as Lady Elmsworth looked on with evident approval. "I would be glad to escort you around the grounds for a time."

Lady Augusta glanced at her mother, who gave her an almost imperceptible nod. Then she looked back towards Stephen and smiled, taking his arm without hesitation.

"I would be glad of your company," she told him, with Lady Elmsworth and Lady Newfield falling into step behind them a short distance away. "Although you need not thank me, Lord Leicestershire. There was nothing difficult about what I did, and certainly no consequences that came thereafter."

"But I must thank you regardless," he answered firmly. "For had you not done so, then I might well have had to deal with a good deal more embarrassment and had the *ton* think all the worse of me." He grimaced. "Someone is certainly eager to do what they can to prevent me from achieving success within society, I am sure of that."

"And we still do not know why," Lady Augusta replied quietly, the smile fading away. "I was very close indeed to discovering who Miss Sidwell was speaking to, only for Lady Villiers to accost me and refuse to allow me from her sight." She sighed and glanced about her. "I do hope that nothing untoward occurs today."

Stephen frowned, opening his mouth to tell Lady Augusta about the woman who had greeted him earlier— only for the very same lady to approach him, cutting directly in front of himself and Lady Augusta as they walked.

"Lord Leicestershire," she said with a hard line about her mouth and a darkness to her eyes. "You are attempting to ignore me, I see."

Stephen's stomach began to churn as he looked at the lady, swallowing hard as he tried desperately to recall her.

He could not do so.

"You may wish to pretend that we are not acquainted, but I shall not permit you to ignore me," she continued, her eyes flashing. "I am under your protection, am I not?"

He felt Lady Augusta stiffen, his breath hitching as he tried to find something to say in response to this. He had no knowledge of this lady and certainly she was not under his protection! Blinking furiously, he cleared his throat and shook his head fervently, one hand held up, palm flat out.

"You are mistaken," he said firmly, aware there were

those around him who were now listening to everything that he said, heat rising within him as he continued to deny their association. "I do not even know your name!"

"How can you deny it?" she cried, her dark hair curling out from under her bonnet, her dark blue eyes flashing as she took a step closer. "I do not appreciate your denials, Lord Leicestershire."

The ache in his throat began to grow steadily, and he looked away, seeing Lady Augusta's eyes flare as she looked up at him. He did not know what to say. This lady clearly knew his name, knew his face, and was able to identify him without too much difficulty, whereas he was quite certain he had never seen her before in his life.

"Lady Claverhouse."

Lady Augusta's voice was tremulous, her hands shaking as she pulled her hand from his arm.

"Lady Augusta," the dark-haired lady said, casting her an inauspicious glance. "I see you are acquainted with Lord Leicestershire."

"Not only acquainted," Lady Augusta said, sharply. "I—"

She cut herself off, darting a look at him before closing her eyes tightly. "What I mean to say, Lady Claverhouse, is that I am *well* acquainted with Lord Leicestershire," she said, a little tightly. "I did not know that you..." Again, she trailed off, clearly uncertain about what to say next. Lady Claverhouse laughed softly, her eyes a little narrowed.

"I do hope you have not been thinking too warmly of Lord Leicestershire, Lady Augusta," she said as Lady

Augusta stood there quietly, unsure as to what else to say. "Especially given this is something of a surprise to you."

"This is a surprise to me also," Stephen interrupted loudly, seeing that there were a good many now watching him. "We are not acquainted, Lady Claverhouse. And I certainly have not once offered you my protection, and nor have I been in receipt of any favors that you might bestow on me thereafter." The warmth in his face grew as he spoke but he did not look away nor try to speak quietly so as to hide what he was saying from others. "You are mistaken, Lady Claverhouse."

She lifted her chin, her eyes flashing. With a set to her jaw, she pulled something from her pocket and held it out to him.

"If that is not the case, Lord Leicestershire, then might you explain how I have come to have *this* in my possession?"

It was as though the entirety of Hyde Park had gone silent in one single moment. Stephen could not see anything but what Lady Claverhouse held up, horrified when she showed him the one thing that he knew for certain he could not deny was his own.

The signet ring that he had lost some days before. The signet ring that he had thought had been knocked from his finger, lost between one person and the next, swept around on the floor by the many feet that trampled upon it. The signet ring that he had lost without any real idea as to where it had gone. The seal upon it was unmistakable—and from the look on Lady Augusta's face, she knew so too.

He shook his head, mute. This could not be. He had never met Lady Claverhouse in his life, but now to see her looking at him with such a pronounced expression made his heart ache with a fierce terror that had his lungs burning as he gasped for air, feeling as though he were being pulled into quicksand, stuck fast with no hope of finding a foothold. There were so many watching him now, so many with their gaze fastened upon him, waiting to hear what he had to say—and yet, he could find nothing of note. His throat was dry, his hands trembling as he shook his head fervently, but even Lady Augusta seemed to be struggling with whether or not she could believe him.

Lady Claverhouse smirked—and at that moment, when he saw the look on her face, Stephen knew that something more was afoot. This was by the same people who had spoken together in the bookshop when Lady Augusta had overheard them. This was more of what had occurred before.

His anger flew through him all at once, catching his breath as he took a step closer, his hand out and one finger out towards Lady Claverhouse. His brows lowered, a line forming there, and when he spoke, his voice was filled with fury.

"Who gave you my ring?"

The smirk disappeared from Lady Claverhouse's face at once and she swallowed hard, looking away for a moment.

"I lost that ring some time ago," he continued, quite certain that his words were carrying out across Hyde Park but finding that he did not care in the least. He was determined to defend himself. "I have been searching for it eagerly and I know all too well that someone must have discovered it and has encouraged you—or employed you in some respect—to ensure that I am brought low yet again. Is that not so?"

Lady Augusta sucked in a breath as he glanced back at her, his brows furrowed still.

"I pray that you would not be taken in by this charlatan," he said to her, his gaze fixed to hers. "Do you not recall that I told you, Lady Augusta, that I lost my signet ring some days ago?" He looked at her steadily, seeing how pale her face was but praying that she would not turn away from him. He needed her now more than ever before, and if she turned her back and said she could not recall what he spoke of, then all would be lost.

Much to his surprise, Lady Newfield came to stand next to Lady Augusta, her eyes fixed to Lady Claverhouse who, after only a moment, ducked her head and turned it away.

"Think of what you know of Lord Leicestershire, Lady Augusta," she said softly, barely loud enough for Stephen to hear. "And do not allow yourself to become distracted by what is before you. You know very well that there are those seeking to injure Lord Leicestershire, do you not?"

"I—I am aware," Lady Augusta answered, her voice quivering just a little as she darted her gaze around the grounds, clearly aware there were, by now, a good many of the *beau monde* watching them. "But if you state that you did lose this ring, Lord Leicestershire, then..." Swallowing hard, Lady Augusta lifted her chin a notch and let out a ragged breath, glancing towards Lady Newfield for just a moment, who then melted back to stand by Lady Elmsworth once more. "Then, I shall trust your word," Lady Augusta finished firmly.

It was as if the trumpets had sounded, such was the swell of relief in Stephen's chest. With a triumphant grin, he turned back to Lady Claverhouse, who was now looking back at him with a grim expression writhing through her features. She was beautiful even in her anger, but there was also a hardness there that Stephen could see etched under her skin. He knew he had come up with the right answer, knew that Lady Claverhouse had been asked to do such a thing by someone else, someone who had been trying to bring his reputation down into the dirt.

"You seek to make excuses simply to protect this...this *chit* from the truth," Lady Claverhouse spat, turning her head away as though Stephen were being nothing other than ridiculous. "You come to me in order to satisfy your desires and, having promised me many trinkets, you gave me this ring in its place until such a time as you could procure them."

Stephen shook his head, reaching out and snatching the signet ring back from Lady Claverhouse.

"That is nothing more than a lie," he stated, his jaw working furiously, "and I will not allow it to stand." Looking all around him, seeing the many faces all turned towards him, watching him openly, he addressed the listening crowd and ignored his embarrassment entirely.

"I have never been acquainted with this lady," he told them all as Lady Claverhouse's face began to flood with color—although, given how her eyebrows were drawn and the hardness in her eyes, Stephen suspected that it was out of anger rather than anything more. "I do not know her. She has my signet ring, yes, but Lady Augusta knows that I spoke to her of my missing ring some days ago. This is all a conspiracy against me, as ridiculous as that may sound." Taking a deep breath, he let the air settle in his chest before he spoke again. "Someone is attempting to ruin my reputation and to have my status in society shattered completely, but I will not allow them to succeed. I will refute every untruth, every single word that is spoken that does not come from honesty and sincerity."

"You cannot believe him!" Lady Claverhouse cried as if they were on the stage and she playing the part of the poor, defenseless creature who had been cast aside without explanation. "I have his signet ring! I am under his protection! There can be no other explanation."

"I would *never* seek out a lady such as yourself," he told her, without any hesitation. "I have no need to do so."

"And I believe him without hesitation," Lady Augusta interrupted, her voice a good deal stronger now, although there was still a pinched look about her face. "Lord Leicestershire is not his brother. Therefore, he is not inclined towards—"

"What does it matter what Lady Augusta thinks?" Lady Claverhouse cried, throwing up her hands as Stephen felt his hands curl into fists, looking at Lady Claverhouse with a dark expression. "She has no bearing on this conversation!"

Stephen drew in a long breath, silence rippling out from him. He felt as though he were standing on the crest of a wave, ready to rush forward, accepting all that would follow from what he was to say. Lady Augusta's head drooped forward, her gaze now on the ground beside his feet. Almost everyone around him stood in silence, looking from one to the next as they waited for him to say something.

"Lady Augusta has a good deal to say on this matter, Lady Claverhouse," he began, his voice quiet but sounding as though it rang out across the park. "She is of great importance to me." He cleared his throat, holding out one hand to Lady Augusta without looking at her. Much to his relief, he felt her touch his hand almost at once, her fingers linking through his. "In fact, Lady Claverhouse, this young lady—this exquisite, beautiful, and exceptional young lady—is my betrothed."

He heard the ripple of astonishment wash out from those around him but did not lift his gaze from Lady Claverhouse, who was now staring at him with wide eyes, clearly either horrified or astonished at what had been said. "Therefore, I care nothing for what society will believe, Lady Claverhouse. If they wish to believe me cruel, unfeeling, selfish, or arrogant, then let them do so. The only opinion I care for is that of Lady Augusta and since she is disinclined to believe you, then I think there can be nothing else to say." He inclined his head but did not drop his eyes, feeling a small sense of satisfaction curl in his stomach as Lady Augusta pressed his hand gently. "If you will excuse us, Lady Claverhouse, we shall continue our walk. Pray do not interrupt us with your nonsense again."

So saying, he turned to the left and began to stride away, with Lady Augusta quickening her steps to keep up with him. He did not look either to the right nor to the left but kept his gaze fixed straight ahead, refusing to catch anyone's eyes for fear of what he might allow to show on his face should he do so.

"Lord Leicestershire," Lady Augusta whispered, her hand still in his. "Might you release me for a moment so that we can walk as we ought?"

He stopped dead, causing Lady Augusta to stumble, her face a little pink. Gently, she put one hand around his arm, and they fell into step together, with Lady Augusta forcing a smile to her lips that Stephen was sure she did not feel. He did not dare to look as to where Lady Elmsworth had gone, afraid of what she might think of him, as well as what she would say once the opportunity was presented to her.

"I am deeply sorry, Lady Augusta," he said as the crowd began to murmur a little more loudly, allowing him to speak with a good deal more openness now. "I should have asked you about your intentions regarding our betrothal. I confess that I have done very little in terms of attempting to bring it to a close, but I ought not to have stated that our engagement now stands without first speaking to you also."

"Lord Leicestershire, please do not trouble yourself." Lady Augusta's hand tightened on his arm for a moment, although she kept her face turned away, her eyes not nearing his own. "I am more than contented with our betrothal, I assure you."

He did not answer for a moment, slowing his steps just a little as he tried to consider what he ought to say or do next. To have spoken so openly, to have made such a decision and spoken it aloud now meant that there could be nothing other than what he had stated between them. There was no opportunity to remove himself now, but Stephen was well aware no such desire lingered within his heart any longer. He *wanted* to be betrothed to Lady Augusta, wanted to marry her and make her his wife. There was a kindness and a compassion to her heart that had him reveling in her company, made him realize what a fool he had been to turn away from her without any true consideration. He had been offended, foolish and arrogant, believing himself to be somehow of greater importance now that he had taken on the title.

Instead, he had been nothing but a fool, lost in the sway of society, who had held him captive and sought to make him believe that they thought more highly of him than any other. Instead, they had turned on him after only a moment, choosing to turn to gossip and rumor, laughing at his misfortune—and only Lady Augusta had chosen to stand by him, to believe that he was not as they thought him. He did not deserve a second chance from her, and yet here she was by his side, accepting their betrothal, agreeing to wed him as had been planned, and all without a word of complaint.

"I think very highly of you, Lady Augusta."

He stopped and turned to face her, ignoring those around them, pushing away the whispers and the shadows that threatened to pull him back. He took her in as though he were seeing her for the first time, seeing her gentle expression, the lightness in her emerald eyes and the tiny crook in the corner of her mouth.

"I should never have told you that I wanted to end our betrothal," he confessed. "I have been nothing more than a fool, believing that I knew best, that the *ton* was eager for my presence among them and thinking that what you sought to tell me, what you were eager to show me, was nothing more than ridiculous." Shaking his head, he dropped his gaze for a moment, letting what he wanted to say make its way from his thoughts to his lips. "Lady Augusta, I would be greatly honored if you would continue to consider us engaged. I swear to you that I shall treat you with all the respect and consideration that you deserve, for I feel myself greatly unworthy of you."

"Then you are quite mistaken," she told him firmly. "You are not at all unworthy, Lord Leicestershire." Her smile grew as she held his gaze, and despite the difficulty of what had occurred with Lady Claverhouse, Stephen believed he saw a true spark of happiness in her features, which overwhelmed him. Could she truly be happy with someone such as he?

"Then I shall send the papers to your father the very moment I return home," he told her, astonished when she practically beamed at him, color mounting in her cheeks in what could only be a blush. "I should have done so a long time ago, Lady Augusta, but I swear that I shall not delay any longer."

"I look forward to our engagement ball, which my father has already arranged for us," she told him with a twinkle in her eye. "Everything is in place—all it now requires is a day and time which will satisfy you."

He laughed, feeling a sudden sense of freedom course through his chest as she smiled at him. "Then it shall be the very next day, if I can manage it," he told her, making her giggle, the sound chasing away the last of his frustration and confusion over Lady Claverhouse. "And mayhap, with this announcement, there will come an end to what has been a very difficult time."

Lady Augusta's smile faded a little. "I must hope so," she answered as he offered her his arm again so that they might be able to walk towards the carriage again, where, Stephen saw, Lady Elmsworth now stood waiting for them, her eyes fixed upon them both. "I do not want you to have any more difficulties."

"Nor I," he agreed, reaching across to pat her hand with his free one. "I cannot tell you how much I value your trust, Lady Augusta. I swear to you, I have no knowledge of Lady Claverhouse."

"I trust your word," she told him, her face set. "Lady Claverhouse is well known to the *ton*. She is often seen with various gentlemen and does not have any qualms about showing off her current...associates." With a slight moue of distaste, she glanced up at him. "But I know you well enough, Lord Leicestershire, to know that you are not a gentleman inclined to doing such a foolish thing, especially not when you are already struggling."

Allowing himself a small, contented smile, Stephen felt his heart lift with happiness at the fresh joy that had come upon him with Lady Augusta's agreement. "Then I am all the more blessed," he said as she smiled at him again. "I look forward to setting a date for our wedding, Lady Augusta, so that we might begin our lives together."

"As do I, Lord Leicestershire," she said, and Stephen found that he had not even the smallest doubt that every word she said was nothing but the truth.

CHAPTER TEN

"And now the ball is this evening!"

Augusta smiled with delight and squeezed her friend's arm gently as they walked together to the shop where she intended to purchase one or two new items to complete her ensemble for the ball.

"It is," she said with a thrill of happiness that ran up her spine. "I am truly glad that all has gone as well."

"As am I," Lady Mary said firmly. "Although we must not tarry too long, else I fear that your mother will begin to become quite frantic!"

Augusta laughed and shook her head. "My mother has become a little ridiculous since the announcement of my engagement," she said, pushing the door open and stepping into the shop, immediately lowering her voice as she did so. "The date was set within a few hours of my returning home, for the papers arrived from Lord Leicestershire, along with a letter to my father expressing his desire for the wedding preparations to begin almost immediately." A warm glow filled her as she remembered all that had occurred, and how eager Lord Leicestershire had been. "Of course, Mama has been a little upset over the rumors regarding Lady Claverhouse, but I have been able to convince her that it is nothing more than Lady Claverhouse seeking to gain some financial gain from Lord Leicestershire, which he refused to give." She shrugged, her fingers tracing a silk ribbon that was resting on the counter, the gentle sheen of the fabric almost begging for her to pick it up. "I told her that his steadfast refusal to give in to Lady Claverhouse meant that he was a gentleman of strong character."

"And she has accepted that?"

"Of course," Augusta confirmed, excitement filling her as she picked up the silk ribbon, wondering if it would look well threaded through her curls that evening. "My father has, of course, continued to give his consent and has no real concerns regarding Lord Leicestershire. They have discussed matters in private and my father is quite happy regarding all the arrangements."

Lady Mary smiled at this, her eyes holding something that made Augusta suspicious, looking at her friend with a slightly narrowed gaze.

"I am glad," Lady Mary said softly, her fingers now tracing the length of the ribbon that Augusta had only just set down. "I do hope you and Lord Leicestershire will find contented happiness together."

Augusta tipped her head. "Might I inquire as to Lord Dryden?" she asked, noting how Lady Mary's head lifted sharply, confirming what she had already suspected. "He has continued being just as attentive?"

Spots of color appeared in Lady Mary's cheeks. "He

has," she admitted without any real hesitation, although she did not look into Augusta's face. "In fact, he has sought permission to court me."

Augusta gasped with delight, reaching out to grasp Lady Mary's hand. "Truly?" she asked as Lady Mary smiled through her blushes. "Then he must truly have excellent intentions for you."

Lady Mary laughed. "Well, of that, I cannot be sure, but I must hope that it will bring me a happiness I have long sought," she said candidly. "He is an honorable gentleman and I find myself more than a little happy with his attention."

"And he is handsome," Augusta added as Lady Mary laughed aloud, turning away and shaking her head at Augusta's teasing. "Well, I shall pray for your happiness to be fulfilled, Lady Mary, for it is the very least that you deserve."

Lady Mary said nothing, although she smiled her thanks as she continued to meander through the shop. There was all manner of things to purchase, from ribbons to silk gloves, to seed pearls and earbobs. Whilst Augusta had her gown already prepared, she wanted very much to find a few extra things that she might pair with her gown for what was sure to be a wonderful evening.

"There she is!"

Augusta frowned at the whisper, hearing the door to the shop close softly behind what was sure to be some gossiping young ladies, all eager to speak to the lady betrothed to Lord Leicestershire. She had endured a good deal of it this last sennight but was now growing rather weary of it all, especially since there had been no other

issues nor matters of concern coming Lord Leicestershire's way since their betrothal announcement had been
made.

"If it is I that you seek, ladies," she said directly,
turning around to see three pairs of eyes widening with
surprise and embarrassment, "then I can assure you that I
have no interest in being gossiped about. I shall say
nothing about Lord Leicestershire to you, save to state
that I am very glad about our engagement and look
forward to our betrothal with a great deal of excitement."
She arched one eyebrow, and the three young ladies
blushed furiously, turning away from her at once. Lady
Mary drew near to Augusta, her brow puckered with
obvious dissatisfaction.

"Mayhap this was not wise," she murmured, but
Augusta waved her concern away at once.

"I am sure there is nothing to concern ourselves
with," she stated loudly enough for the three other ladies
to hear. "I have had more than a few members of the *ton*
seeking me out so that they might hear what I have to say
on what has occurred and thereafter, spreading it through
society as though they have every right to know my inner-
most thoughts." She shrugged, her eyes still hard as she
kept her gaze pinned to the three young ladies' backs. "I
shall not be intimidated nor kept away from town
because of idle chatter."

Lady Mary's frown flickered and then lifted slowly,
her expression turned a little brighter. "I must confess
that I am still somewhat concerned that any of those who
draw near to you are the ones who have been attempting
to ruin Lord Leicestershire," Lady Mary explained as

Augusta nodded. "I do wish that we could discover the truth as to their reasons for doing so."

Augusta shrugged and then settled her shoulders, her lips a little pinched. "I believe that those responsible have had no other choice but to bring their campaign to a swift conclusion," she said, even though, were she honest, she would have admitted to herself that she was on tenter-hooks whenever she had gone out into society these last few days. "Given I am engaged to Lord Leicestershire and have no intention whatsoever of ending our betrothal, there is no need for them to continue as they have been. Bringing Lord Leicestershire's reputation into the mud will do them no good."

"That is true, I suppose," Lady Mary agreed a little hesitantly. "But still, it is somewhat unsettling to be entirely unaware of who was attempting to do so in the first place."

Augusta nodded, glancing at the three young ladies as they hurried from the shop, clearly a little embarrassed by what she had said to them. "That is true, of course," she agreed. "But there is little benefit in continuing to allow my thoughts to linger upon such a thing, not when there is a wedding to plan."

At this, Lady Mary let out a long, wistful sigh, clearly no longer caught up in thoughts that worried her. "Yes, indeed," she replied, picking up the ribbon again. "I am very much looking forward to this evening, as I am sure you are, Lady Augusta."

Augusta smiled and picked up the small silk ribbon and then took the second from Lady Mary's fingers. "Come then; let us purchase both of these and we shall both look quite wonderful this evening." Stalling Lady Mary's protests with a quiet laugh, she squeezed her friend's fingers and then took them to the shopkeeper, her heart filled with joy and anticipation for what she was certain would be a wonderful evening.

THE START of the evening had gone as wonderfully as Augusta had expected. She had been a little afraid that there had been too many rumors and too much gossip and that those in the *ton* might refuse to attend—but what she had realized soon afterward was that the *beau monde* reveled in such things and thus, she had not been surprised to see the guests pouring in.

But what had been the most wonderful thing of all was seeing Lord Leicestershire walking into the room, his eyes searching for her amongst the crowd. As she had stood there, watching him, she had felt her heart fill with anticipation, waiting for him to see her, and as he had finally found her in the crowd, something like giddiness had overcome her entirely, making her heart throw itself into her chest and her breath hitch. Warmth had spread from the tips of her fingers to the very ends of her toes, and now, as she waltzed in his arms, Augusta knew that there was more than just a gentle regard for him within her heart.

There was a deep affection for Lord Leicestershire now, her heart practically filled with him. He was endeared to her now, lodged steadfastly within her heart, mind, and soul until she could not even think of anything other than him.

"You are more beautiful this evening than I think I have ever seen you, Lady Augusta."

His words were like honey, sweet to her lips as she smiled up at him.

"And you are all the more handsome," she teased, seeing how he flushed, his eyes darting away from hers for a moment. She wondered if he felt something for her in the same way that she felt something for him, if there was anything other than regard in his heart. Was there a hope that there might be a love match between them? It was not something she had ever expected, not something she had even hoped for when it came to Lord Leicestershire, but now that they had been through so much together, had endured such a great deal, there might be something between them that could not be easily broken.

"And now I am to set you free to dance with another," Lord Leicestershire murmured as the music came to a close, the couples coming to a stop. "How unfortunate."

She laughed softly, her eyes bright. "But only for a few minutes," she replied, curtsying. "And then I shall be by your side once more."

He offered her his arm. "That cannot come soon enough," he answered meaningfully before he led her from the floor. Lady Mary and Lord Dryden were standing waiting for them, their smiles warm, although a knowing look was exchanged between them as Augusta approached.

"You appeared to be enjoying your dance very

much," Lady Mary commented with a small wink to Augusta. "I was sorry to have missed the waltz."

"Oh?"

Lady Mary rolled her eyes. "My mother insisted on introducing me to a Baron," she said as Lord Dryden chuckled. "It is as if, now that Lord Dryden has shown an interest in me, she is hopeful that I might garner a little more attention from other gentlemen."

Lord Dryden laughed again as Lady Mary blushed. "It is as though she expects me to remove my interest from you and to find someone better," he said, his words directed towards Lady Mary rather than anyone else, turning towards her so that he might look directly into her eyes. "Which, Lady Mary, I can assure you will never occur."

"That is my sentiment also," Lord Leicestershire replied, looking towards Augusta, "although I fear that I am less eloquent than Lord Dryden!"

Smiling softly, Augusta held Lord Leicestershire's gaze for a long moment, before she caught sight of someone approaching from the shadows. For a moment, she saw another figure watching him approach, but it was gone in an instant, leaving her to focus on the gentleman making his way towards her. A sigh escaped her, and her smile dropped from her lips, aware now that she was to be taken to the dance floor by another.

"Lord Drake," she said, trying to smile at him but finding the thought of being apart from Lord Leicestershire difficult. "The country dance, is it not?"

"The quadrille," he corrected her, bowing, although

she noted that he staggered slightly as he did so. "Shall we take to the floor, Lady Augusta?"

Augusta hesitated, seeing Lord Leicestershire frown and feeling the same hesitation in herself. Lord Drake appeared to have enjoyed a little too much of the champagne already, even though it was early in the evening. She did not want him to tread on her toes, did not want him to embarrass her on what was her wonderful evening. And yet, she had accepted a dance from him and had not noticed the state of him at the time.

"Lady Augusta?"

"Yes, yes," she said before she could think of an acceptable excuse to remove herself. "Thank you, Lord Drake. Yes, of course. The quadrille."

His hand was rough as he grasped hers, placing it on his arm before she could do so herself. Augusta jerked away from him and walked by herself towards the dance floor, a step or two ahead of Lord Drake. When he finally came to stand beside her, she found him swaying to one side and then the other, making her move back from him all the more.

A strange sensation came over her as she looked up at him, a little anxious. Glancing over her shoulder, she saw Lord Leicestershire watching her with sharp eyes, although his gaze soon shifted towards Lord Drake instead of to herself. Even with the distance between them, she could read the anxiety in his face, clearly a little worried about Lord Drake just as she herself was.

"Are you quite certain that you feel able to do so, Lord Drake?" she asked as the music began to play across the room, swelling louder and louder as the introduction came to a close and the couples came to stand together. "Are you feeling well enough to do so?"

Instead of answering her, Lord Drake pulled her into his arms and began to dance, finally separating from her a beat too late. She was a little off-balance, struggling to find her place and finding herself more than a little reluctant to step back into Lord Drake's arms. He was laughing uproariously, as though she were doing something worthy of such mirth, only to hold her a little too tightly, crushing her against him. By the time the end of the dance came, she was breathless and confused, finding it very difficult to keep her place given Lord Drake was making a mess of the dance in its entirety. When she curtsied, it was with nothing more than relief, glad that she would be soon removed from the dance floor and back beside Lord Leicestershire.

"Ah, Lady Augusta," Lord Drake said, lurching forward as he grasped her arm. "I must apologize for my lack of skill in this particular dance."

"I think it best that you mayhap spare the next young lady the difficulty of having to keep in step with you, Lord Drake," she told him bluntly. "Now, shall we perhaps return to the others?" She began to step forward, only for Lord Drake to grasp her arm, a dark look on his face. The stumbling and lurching came to an immediate stop and his eyes became focused and narrowed, looking down at her with a renewed sense of purpose.

And then, he was leaning down, his head close to hers—and before she knew what she was doing, Augusta had stumbled back, only for Lord Drake to grasp her arm tightly and pull her back towards him. Her heart was in her throat, her breath rasping out of her as she struggled to remove herself from him, fearful of what his intentions were. When his head lowered again, she reached out with one hand and pushed him back, only for his fingers to dig into her arm. When his head neared hers again, when he pulled her closer, Augusta did the only thing she could manage.

She slapped him hard, the sound seeming to resonate around the room. Lord Drake stumbled back, his hand pressed to his face and shock rippling across his features. Then, out of nowhere, Lord Leicestershire was beside them, pulling her back, whilst Lord Dryden and Lady Mary practically flew at Lord Drake, pushing him away from her.

"Lady Augusta!" Lord Leicestershire was searching her face, his eyes filled with a mixture of anger and concern. "Are you all right? Lady Augusta!"

She blinked, aware now that she was in the corner of the ballroom without having any real knowledge of how she had come to be there. "Yes, yes," she managed to whisper, shock rippling over her as she realized what had almost occurred. "I am quite all right, although I do not understand..." Closing her eyes, she breathed long and hard, trying to overcome the shock that came over her.

"Lord Drake was attempting to kiss you," Lord Leicestershire muttered, raking one hand through his hair. "I cannot understand why, other than to say that he was in his cups and clearly had very little thought as to what he was doing."

Augusta closed her eyes tightly, glad to hear the music for the next dance beginning and praying that not everyone was now watching her but fully aware whispers would already be starting. No doubt, by the end of the night, every single guest present would take what they had seen and be ready to speak of it to each of their acquaintances.

"I thought him a little overcome but did not think him to be so foolish," she whispered, holding out her hand and feeling Lord Leicestershire grasp it tightly. Drawing strength from him, she forced herself to open her eyes, feeling the room spin as she tried to focus on his face. "I cannot understand why he would attempt to do so."

Lord Leicestershire's face changed in an instant. His eyes widened, his face became pale, and his hand tightened on hers. She stared at him, her heart thumping furiously as she looked back at him, silently trying to encourage him to say whatever it was that had come to his mind.

"I pray that this is not to do with me," he said, his voice much lower and his expression darkening with every moment. "This could not be an attempt to bring shame to me by doing such a thing to you?"

A tremor ran through her as she let what he had said run through her mind, considering it carefully. Could it be true? Could someone have attempted to have her ruined by society, even though the fault would not have been hers but rather Lord Drake's? She had seen it many times before, when a gentleman had behaved in a poor and despicable fashion only for the consequences to fall upon whatever young lady had the misfortune of being involved.

"It would make sense," she whispered, her fingers tightening on his. "Just before he attempted to do such a thing, Lord Drake's expression cleared." Swallowing hard, she recalled the fright that had run through her as she had looked up into Lord Drake's expression and seen a clearness to his eyes that told her he was not as drunk as she had first thought. It had been a deliberate act, she noted, her breath shuddering out of her as she closed her eyes once more.

"Then we must discover the truth, as we have attempted to do before," Lord Leicestershire said with a heaviness to his voice that had her opening her eyes, wanting to reach for him, to let herself drift into him and gain strength from his presence there. Instead, she simply nodded and tried to push away the feeling of weakness that had overcome her. Gaining a little more strength from the look in Lord Leicestershire's face, she drew in a deep breath and set her shoulders.

"We should discuss the matter in its entirety," she said as she saw her father coming towards her, his brows low over his eyes and his jaw working furiously. A little behind him came Lord Dryden and Lady Mary, both of whom wore an expression of outrage. Their eyes were blazing fire, their faces heated and a firmness to their mouth that told her they were deeply upset on her behalf.

"Father," she said, letting go of Lord Leicestershire's hand and reaching out towards her father. "I am quite all right."

"The cad!" her father exclaimed as Lord Leicestershire came to stand next to her, his hand on the small of her back. "I have had him thrown from the house in disgrace, of course." His eyes searched her face and Augusta tried to smile, wanting to reassure her father that she was not at all injured in any way. "If he had managed to succeed, then I do not know what would have occurred." His eyes moved towards Lord Leicestershire as though seeing him for the first time, a flicker of doubt making its way into his expression.

"There is nothing to concern yourself with, Lord Elmsworth," she heard Lord Leicestershire say as she looked up at her betrothed. "I do not hold Lady Augusta responsible for anything that occurred here this evening and, had the worst happened, you would not have found me breaking our engagement. I care for your daughter very much and look forward to our wedding all the more."

Augusta found her smile to be a genuine one at this remark, her heart pushing through the shock and the cold that had clasped it tightly ever since Lord Drake had attempted to kiss her. It began to wash from her heart as Lady Mary came towards her, murmuring her apology for not stepping forward sooner. Augusta waved this away and reassured her friend that it was quite all right, pressing her father's hand for just a moment as he turned to take his leave of them.

"The foolish man ought not to have drunk so much champagne," Lady Mary said with a firm shake of her head. "To be in his cups so early in the evening is almost unforgivable!"

"I do not think he was in his cups at all," Augusta replied, making Lady Mary and Lord Dryden look at her in surprise. "It was an act."

Lord Leicestershire nodded, clearing his throat before he spoke. "I would be inclined to agree," he said, with Lord Dryden frowning hard at this remark. "From what Lady Augusta has stated, it appears as though Lord Drake intended to do such a thing purposefully, to bring shame to both her and consequentially, to myself."

"But why?" Lady Mary asked, only to screw up her eyes as she shut them tightly, waving a few fingers. "Yes, of course. I see why you would think such a thing." Opening her eyes, she let out a long breath and shook her head. "The same persons who sought to bring you shame and disgrace, Lord Leicestershire, are continuing to do so but now also include Lady Augusta, since she is engaged to you."

Lord Dryden's frown lifted. "Or to bring your engagement to an end by one means or the next."

Augusta resisted the urge to rub at her forehead in frustration, wishing she could understand who had done such a thing and why. "If only I could have caught a glimpse of them in the bookshop that afternoon," she said heavily, her shoulders drooping. "Then none of this might have occurred."

To her surprise, Lord Leicestershire slipped one hand about her waist and pulled her close. She looked up at him, her breath catching as he gazed down at her, his eyes warm and his expression almost joyous.

"But then we might not find ourselves as we are now," he reminded her, making her blush as heat spiraled up from her chest and into her heart. "And that would be rather dire indeed, would it not?"

There was no denying that what he said was true,

and thus, Augusta had no other choice but to agree, her cheeks reddening as she nodded, unable to find the words to express what was within her own heart—particularly not in front of Lady Mary and Lord Dryden!

"It is as though I have stepped out of the shadows and into the light," he told her, turning towards her a little more so that he might speak with openness, as Lord Dryden and Lady Mary looked away. "As if I—"

"The shadows!" Augusta grasped Lord Leicestershire's hand with tight fingers, staring up at him with wide eyes, something about the shadows burning into her mind yet remaining unclear. Lord Dryden and Lady Mary stared at her, with Lady Mary taking a small step closer to her, as though to encourage her to recall whatever it was that she was trying so desperately to remember.

"Lady Augusta?" Lord Leicestershire murmured, his eyes searching her face, his free hand now coming to clasp over the top of their joined ones. "What is it?"

"The shadows," she whispered, one hand pressed to her stomach as she tried desperately to recall what it was she had seen. "When Lord Drake approached me, there was someone watching him, as though he had spoken to them and then come to take me to dance. Someone who..." She caught her breath, one hand pressed tightly against her stomach as she saw a face beginning to appear. "It was one of the guests present this evening, of course. A young lady."

Lord Leicestershire's hands tightened for a moment, a flash of excitement flooding his eyes. "Do you recall her face well, Lady Augusta?" he asked, clearly desperate for her to know who she had seen. "Do you remember anything specific about her features?"

Try as she might, Augusta could not remember anything specific, other than the recollection that it had been a young lady watching Lord Drake from the shadows. Shaking her head, she let out a long, exasperated breath, wishing desperately that she could remember the face.

"A young lady, then," Lady Mary said with such a sense of firmness that Augusta was surprised. "That is something, at least!" She smiled at Augusta encouragingly, but Augusta could only sigh. "You must not be frustrated with yourself, Augusta," Lady Mary continued. "You have remembered something and that, I am sure, will be very helpful indeed. A young lady of quality is, in some way, involved in what has occurred with Lord Leicestershire and with you."

Lord Dryden cleared his throat. "And she will need to be acquainted with Lord Drake, with Lady Whitaker, Miss Sidwell—was that her name?" With a small nod in Lord Leicestershire's direction, Lord Dryden continued. "And she might well have been acquainted with Miss Hartnett also, although I cannot say that I believe that Miss Harnett was in any way involved in what happened to her."

"That is a wise assumption," Lord Leicestershire agreed, "although I—"

His expression changed in an instant, the words dying on his lips as he stared blankly ahead, his fingers loosening on Augusta's. Her heart began to quicken at the look in his eyes, at the way he caught his breath, his eyes wide and staring as though he had only just come to realize something. No one spoke. No one said even a single word as they all waited for Lord Leicestershire to explain what had just occurred.

And then, he let out a harsh bark of laughter.

"My goodness," he said, hoarsely, shaking his head and running one hand over his eyes. "Can it be? Can it truly be her?" With another wry shake of his head, he looked first at Augusta and then at Lady Mary and Lord Dryden, evidently seeing the look of hopeful anticipation on each of their faces. Letting out another hard laugh, he reached out and touched Augusta's cheek, his eyes a little cold.

"I have it now," he told her softly. "I believe I know who has done all of this, although what her reasons are to be, I cannot understand."

"Who is it?" she asked eagerly, only to be thoroughly disappointed as Lord Leicestershire shook his head.

"Would that I could tell you, but I believe that for the present, it is better if it remain within my own heart and mind," he told her, the look in his eyes almost begging her to trust him. "Tomorrow, however, all shall become clear." With a long breath, he set his shoulders. "Lady Mary, might you ask Miss Sidwell to meet you tomorrow afternoon?" He spread out one hand, shrugging. "Simply ask her to join you for a walk into town, and then make your way to the bookshop where Lady Augusta first overheard those two ladies speak."

Augusta turned her gaze to Lady Mary, seeing her eyes wide and her mouth open and close again, only for her friend to nod and remain otherwise entirely silent.

"Very good," Lord Leicestershire said firmly. "Then Lord Dryden, you shall have to drag Lord Drake to that bookshop also, although I do not particularly care how you do so." He chuckled at the wry grin that spread across Lord Dryden's face, before turning to Augusta. "And you, my dear Lady Augusta, might you be willing to bring Lady Whitaker?"

Augusta wrinkled her nose, not at all inclined towards the lady but agreed without hesitation. "If you wish her to be present, then I shall, of course, do as you ask," she told him as Lord Leicestershire lifted her hand to his lips and pressed a kiss to it, making her glow with a deep sense of happiness and joy that chased the rest of her uncertainty and confusion away.

"I thank you," he told her, with eyes that held her gaze intensely, a promise written there that she could not fully make out. "I shall speak to the proprietor and gain the use of the premises for a short time—but I can assure you, Lady Augusta, that by this time tomorrow, the entire mystery will be at an end and there will be nothing to hold us back any longer."

She sighed contentedly, his thumb running over the back of her hand. "Then let us go and enjoy the rest of this evening, Lord Leicestershire," she said as Lady Mary and Lord Dryden turned to lead the way back into the heart of the ballroom. "For tomorrow cannot come quickly enough."

It had all become so very clear to him, Stephen thought to himself, allowing a small smile to catch the corners of his mouth. Walking up and down the bookshop, he waited eagerly for those he had invited to walk inside, knowing full well that those he himself had asked to attend would be the very last to step within.

How close they had come to disaster! With Lord Drake's roguish behavior last evening, he had felt the scandal brushing at both himself and Lady Augusta with its fingertips, shuddering as he thought of it. Lord Drake had something of a roguish reputation, and Stephen was quite certain that he would not have hesitated to do as he had been asked, regardless of the consequences. Consequences that Lady Augusta would have borne.

He had spent almost all of the previous night awake, trying to work out what had occurred and why. He had tried and failed to understand the purposes of the lady's campaign against him, had been unable to discover the truth as to why she had done such things, and yet he had not been able to release such thoughts from his mind in order to give himself a little respite. He was desperately eager to discover the truth, wanted to find out why she had done such things so that he might finally be relieved of his burdens for good. And then, he could look forward to a future with Lady Augusta that would not have even a smudge of difficulty about it. There would be no one holding him back, keeping him wondering about what they might do next. He would be able to give his full attention to Lady Augusta—a lady who had come to mean a good deal more to him than he had ever expected.

You care for her.

The whisper in his heart did not surprise him nor did he refuse to acknowledge it. It was the truth, of course, and he was glad to accept it and hold it as his own. There was a deep affection within his own heart for Lady Augusta now. There was a respect combined with a warm regard that he did not think would ever leave him. Instead, Stephen believed that it would only continue to grow as their relationship blossomed all the more.

He could not have ever imagined being this fond of the lady, given their first meeting! They had both made very poor impressions at the first but now that such things were gone, set aside in the past, he was able to look at her and see her for the beautiful, strong, and determined lady that she was. He was beyond blessed to have found her as his bride. To hold back the betrothal papers, to revel in the attentions of society instead of seeking her attentions had been nothing short of senseless. She had shown him more kindness than he deserved, and he would always be grateful to her for that.

The urge to take her in his arms and kiss her soundly had been almost overwhelming last evening. Even though Lord Drake and Lady Mary had been present, even though the ball was still in full swing, he had wanted to do that very thing. The desire to give in to such an urging had taken a good deal of his strength to battle. But that desire would be satisfied before too long, he told himself, pressing his lips together firmly as he waited for the door to the bookshop to open.

Stephen did not have long to wait. After another minute of pacing up and down, the door opened and Lady Mary stepped inside, laughing at something that her companion—Miss Sidwell—had said. The smile left her face and her eyes became serious the moment she stepped through the door, leaving Miss Sidwell to follow after her. Miss Sidwell was looking all about the bookshop before her gaze finally rested on Stephen, her mouth opening and closing in fright, her eyes wide and her cheeks losing their color. She made for the door, only for Lady Mary to step in front of it.

"My mother is waiting for us in the carriage," Lady Mary told him as Miss Sidwell turned back around to face him, her expression now one of sheer horror as though she expected him to attack her in one way or the other. "Her eyes are fixed upon the door, and it was all I could do to allow us to step inside without her!"

"I thank you," Stephen said graciously, bowing quickly to Miss Sidwell. "Miss Sidwell, I have a few things I must ask you and Lady Mary here was more than willing to help me."

"You are able to speak to me at any time, Lord Leicestershire," the lady replied with as much dignity as she could muster. "Why such duplicity?" There was a quaver to her voice that did not make him believe that she was anything other than afraid, although quite what she feared, he did not yet know.

"Because," he said softly, gesturing to the door as it opened. "I am seeking to speak to not only you, but to one or two others also."

Just as he said such a thing, Lord Drake wandered inside, his brow lowered and his forehead puckered. He glared at Stephen as he walked in, with Lord Dryden only a few steps behind him. Stephen could not help but chuckle at the grin on Lord Dryden's face, wondering what it was the gentleman had said to Lord Drake to convince him that he must attend. No doubt, Lord Dryden had been able to discover some unfortunate rumors or the like about the fellow and had promised to make the truth come to light if Lord Drake did not obey.

"Good afternoon," Stephen told Lord Drake, who ignored him completely. "And now we wait for...ah! Lady Augusta." The door opened again, and Lady Augusta walked inside, her hand on the arm of another lady. Lady Whitaker's eyes flared with astonishment as Lady Augusta led her inside, coming to a dead stop just as the door shut behind her.

"There can be no escape now, Lady Whitaker," Lord Dryden said lazily, coming to stand by the door and folding his arms across his chest as he looked at her. "Do come in. There are a few seats for you to sit down in if the shock of this has been too great." He laughed harshly and Stephen saw the look of fear flash into Lady Whitaker's eyes as she took in the other two guests who were present. Evidently, she knew now that he made the connection between them all and understood precisely what had occurred. He smiled wolfishly to himself as she glanced at him, his own brows lowering as he looked around the room. Lady Augusta had not come near to him, knowing that he would need to speak to all of those present and not wanting to interrupt his thoughts by her closeness. He appreciated her all the more for that.

"There is but one opportunity for you all to speak the truth, and that is all the opportunity you shall have," he began, speaking loud enough for his voice to fill the room. "I believe I know it all, but you are required to confirm it."

Lord Drake snorted. "And if we prefer to remain silent?"

Lord Dryden pushed himself a little away from the door and cleared his throat, arching one eyebrow and looking steadfastly back at Lord Drake. Stephen did not have to say even a single word, for Lord Drake lowered his head and dropped his gaze, his arrogance evaporating in a moment.

"Miss Sidwell," Stephen continued when Lord Drake lapsed into silence. "I am certain that a few choice words could be shared with your father about what you have chosen to involve yourself in." He saw her blink rapidly, her eyes welling up, but forced himself to feel no sympathy. "That is, unless you speak with honesty. And you, Lady Whitaker." He turned to the lady, who was looking back at him with a hard look in her eyes, which he returned with one of his own. "What would Lord

Whitaker do should he discover that you have been seeking out some rather *close* acquaintances of late, of whom I am one?" He did not smile but saw her shrink into herself, her eyes dropping to the floor, her head low. "I will ask you all some questions and I must know the truth before we can continue. Once you have told me it, there is nothing more that I will ask of you."

Lady Augusta was watching him carefully, and he smiled at her, seeing the tiniest quirk of her mouth as she responded. It was clear to him that she was eager to hear what they each had to say, and to know the truth of it, and he had no reason to wait any longer. His final guest was to arrive in only a few minutes, and he had to have some answers from those present before she did so.

"Lady Whitaker," he said softly, as the lady dared a glance at him before lowering her eyes again. "Might I surmise that you were involved in all of this with the hope that I might, thereafter, come to be one of your *closer* acquaintances?" He held his gaze fixed to her features, but the lady did not look at him. "You were asked to involve yourself in some way, promised that when I was surrounded by the shame and mortification that society's rebuke would bring me, I would then turn to you without hesitation. Or was it more than that?" He narrowed his gaze just a little and as Lady Whitaker sighed heavily, he felt his heart quicken just a little in his chest. What was it she was about to say?

"My husband is not as wealthy as he once was," Lady Whitaker muttered darkly. "That is all."

"I see," Lady Augusta interrupted before he could speak. "So you were involved in setting the trap with

Miss Hartnett simply so that you could try to gain some financial and perhaps personal gain." Her brow was low, a groove between her brows and a spot of red in each cheek, although her voice remained steady and without inflection.

Lady Whitaker shrugged, sighed, and looked away. "Miss Hartnett was not chosen by me," she said, as though that relieved some of her guilt. "She was just unfortunate enough to be chosen."

A beat of silence followed this explanation before Stephen cleared his throat, ready to continue.

"And you, Miss Sidwell," he began, turning to the young lady who was, at this point, now looking more than a little terrified. "Might I ask why you deliberately pretended that you and I were to dance the waltz when it was not true in the least?" He lifted his chin and stared down at her, with Miss Sidwell pressing one hand to her heart and the other to her lips, as if terrified about what he was asking her. "You changed my name from one dance to the next and then sought another gentleman for the dance that I had initially written down, Miss Sidwell," he continued, when she said nothing. "Why?"

Miss Sidwell began to cry, her tears rippling down her cheeks in an instant, but Stephen did not look away nor relinquish his control of the situation. Instead, he simply continued to gaze at her, praying that Lady Augusta and Lady Mary would not give in to her tears and ask him to relent.

They did not.

"Miss Sidwell," he said again when she pulled a handkerchief from her pocket and dabbed at her eyes.

"Might I suggest that you speak to me about what occurred?"

"I did not know what to do!"

Miss Sidwell drew in a shaky breath, her eyes closing tightly. "You were not meant to step in, Lady Augusta. You were supposed to be deeply upset at Lord Leicestershire's behavior, and thereafter, I was to make a very loud exclamation as to his ungentlemanly behavior and..."

"And have the *ton* think all the more poorly of me," he finished for her, as she gave him a jerky nod. "You were convinced to do such a thing very easily, it seems." He tilted his head and looked at her steadily, not asking her anything particular but waiting for her to speak. She let out a long sigh, closing her eyes and swaying just a little, trembling slightly.

"I did so out of fear," she admitted hoarsely. "She is so easily accepted by the *ton* and I knew very well that she could easily do as she threatened."

"What did she threaten?" Stephen asked, knowing that it was only he that was fully aware as to who Miss Sidwell spoke of, with Lord Dryden, Lady Mary, and Lady Augusta still confused. "Did she state that she would have you flung from society?"

Miss Sidwell nodded and began to cry in earnest now, and from the look on Lady Mary's face, Stephen knew that she wanted to comfort the young lady somewhat. Giving her a small nod, he turned to Lord Drake, who was scowling hard.

"I have sympathy for Miss Sidwell," Stephen told him as Lord Drake smirked darkly. "She was forced into doing as she was asked out of fear for what would follow if she did not. You, however, did so because you thought it would be enjoyable to watch what came out of your actions, did you not?"

Lord Drake said nothing for a long moment. He returned Stephen's hard gaze with one of his own, sighing heavily and rolling his eyes before he finally spoke.

"The lady is very lovely," he said as though this was some explanation. "When she explained what she wanted me to do, then I saw no reason *not* to do so." One shoulder lifted. "I am known as a rake and I do not care what society thinks of me."

"And you were to gain nothing from this?" Stephen asked, only for Lord Drake to look away suddenly, making Stephen frown. "What was it you were promised, Lord Drake?"

Again, there came that thick silence that covered them all, with Lord Drake steadfastly refusing to meet his gaze. It was only when Lady Augusta took a step forward, looking pointedly at Lord Drake, followed soon after by Lord Dryden, that Lord Drake finally let out a long breath and spoke. It was dull and monotonous, as though he were reading something from a book that did not hold even a single flicker of interest for him.

"I was asked to do so with the promise that I would, thereafter, be given the opportunity to further my acquaintance with a particular lady that I have had a specific interest in," he said, his expression blank. "A lady who has, thus far, rejected my advances but is well acquainted with Miss Trevelyan. Therefore, she promised that she would be well able to encourage such a connection."

Stephen smiled darkly at Lord Drake, well aware of the gasps of astonishment that had rung out from the others in the room. "Miss Trevelyan has been more than a little involved in all of this, has she not?" he said softly, with a small smile towards Lady Augusta, who was staring at him with wide eyes. "I recalled that Lord Drake had been in Miss Trevelyan's company when I had spoken to her at the park, and thereafter, I recalled that she had been upset with me when I could not remember her name. It appears as though she has taken great offense to my lack of interest in her and has decided to take her revenge. I am certain that Lady Claverhouse is also known to her, although I am not certain what she did to ensure that Lady Claverhouse did as she was asked."

Lord Drake snorted, and everyone turned to him as one, looking at him in surprise. Lord Drake's grim smile lingered, his gaze roving about the group.

"Lady Claverhouse is easily turned by the promise of coin," he told them all as Lord Dryden shook his head in evident astonishment. "Therefore, I am sure that she was given a significant sum for her little performance." He tilted his head and looked at Stephen with eyes like flint. "A performance that was only confirmed when you turned away from Miss Trevelyan without explanation, Lord Leicestershire."

Stephen shook his head. "I have no interest in Miss Trevelyan," he said firmly. "My interest has always been in Lady Augusta, even though I have not always been fully aware of it myself." Catching Lady Augusta's eye, he smiled at her and held her gaze. "Miss Trevelyan has, for whatever reason, wanted to garner my attention solely for her and has attempted to ruin my reputation when I did not turn to her as she expected."

The door opened just as he spoke, and Miss Trevelyan appeared in the doorway, arrested with surprise. Behind her came her mother, who pushed into Miss Trevelyan and forced her forward.

The door swung back tightly, leaving Miss Trevelyan and her mother standing together, staring at the small gathered group with horror-struck expressions on each of their faces. Lord Dryden resumed his position by the door, blocking it so that there was no other choice but for them to remain within.

"Ah, Miss Trevelyan," Stephen said, bowing low. "And Lady Villiers. Do come in and tell us all why you have both been pursuing such a vendetta against me." He put on a tight smile, gesturing with one hand as he waited for one or both of them to speak. The two ladies stared back at him, both white-faced and horrified, clearly having not expected anything of the sort.

"When I approached you last evening, Miss Trevelyan," Stephen continued when she did not speak, "I begged you to meet me here this afternoon and to bring your mother with you. Did you think that I was finally to do as you had long hoped? As *you*, Lady Villiers, had planned?" He shook his head, aware of how Lady Augusta now stared at the two ladies, slowly putting the pieces together. "You intended Miss Trevelyan for me, did you not?"

"And why not?" Lady Villiers exclaimed, striding forward and pointing one hand out towards him. "Your brother promised himself to my daughter and then disappeared back to his estate for a full year without even a single word of his engagement!"

Stephen swallowed hard, feeling a wave of surprise crashing over him. He had never once expected to hear anything related to his brother and certainly had never once been told that there was any such arrangement between his brother and Miss Trevelyan.

"You pretend that you know nothing of it," Lady Villiers spat, her eyes as hard as ice, scraping against him. "But he was your brother! How could you not know that he was promised to my daughter?"

Regaining himself a little, Stephen shook his head. "There was nothing in his papers, Lady Villiers," he told her as steadily as he could. "And my brother and I did not share a great deal of our lives with each other." Tilting his head, he looked down at the lady, suddenly feeling a little unsure of what had been said. "This agreement you speak of...?"

"There were no papers," Miss Trevelyan said, her voice a little tremulous but her eyes as cold as her mother's. "The late Lord Leicestershire stole my affections and then promised that he would return to London so that we might become engaged."

"And he did not do so," Lady Augusta interrupted, coming to stand next to Stephen. "You have mentioned to me before, Lord Leicestershire, that your brother had not come into society for some time and that it had surprised you somewhat."

Stephen nodded slowly, his gaze fixed to Miss Trevelyan, who appeared to be trembling—although whether from anger or upset, he could not say.

"My brother might have promised you something, Miss Trevelyan, but that does not mean that I should take his place," he said slowly. "You should have spoken to me of this supposed verbal agreement between you both and then I could have—"

"And have you laugh such a thing off?" Miss Trevelyan exclaimed, throwing her hands up into the air. "You would have simply turned away from me at once, refusing to accept even a single shred of responsibility. And left me as an outcast, turning away from me entirely."

"So instead, you sought to manipulate Lord Leicestershire towards you, Miss Trevelyan," Lady Augusta said softly, her hand reaching up to rest on his arm. "When he forgot your name, when he turned towards me instead of towards you—all of those deserved a punishment, did they not?"

Miss Trevelyan glowered at Lady Augusta, but Stephen knew instantly from her silence that she had hit upon the truth.

"How did you find my ring?" he asked quietly as Miss Trevelyan's eyes flashed. "Where did you get it from?"

"You fell," Miss Trevelyan said with a shrug. "It was not intended that we find it but when you *unfortunately* fell upon poor Miss Hartnett, your ring fell from your finger. I could not simply return it to you, not when it would work so well for what I required."

Stephen's jaw worked hard. "You sought to punish me for my treatment of you, whilst intending that, if society turned from me, you would then swoop in and stand by me, endearing yourself to me so that you could gain what you always intended, even if there was a small amount of shame to bear for a short time."

Miss Trevelyan's face turned crimson, her hand shaking as she pointed one finger out towards him. "I am meant to be a marchioness!" she cried, her eyes blazing with fury. "You cannot take such a thing from me!"

He shook his head. "And thus, you and your mother spoke together about such a thing whilst you waited for Lady Whitaker to come and join you in this bookshop," he said as Miss Trevelyan turned her furious glare towards Lady Augusta. "Unfortunately, my dear Lady Augusta was present that afternoon and heard some of what was said. When she came to me, I foolishly ignored her—and to my cost." Shaking his head, he pressed his free hand over Lady Augusta's where it rested on his arm, smiling down at her. "And then we came together, our betrothal renewed and a fresh determination in our hearts."

"A determination that has led us to the truth," Lady Augusta said, her voice filled with a newfound strength. "Miss Trevelyan, you have sought to take something that would never have been yours. Lord Leicestershire and I have been betrothed for some time and, whilst I feared that it might never come to be, it is now without doubt that we shall wed and spend our lives as husband and wife." She looked up at him, her expression one of sheer joy. "And I can hardly wait for such a thing."

"Nor I," he agreed, glancing back at Miss Trevelyan and seeing the color fade from her face. "Lady Villiers, Miss Trevelyan, you have both behaved with cruelty and selfishness, but you have not succeeded. Miss Trevelyan will never be my marchioness, for she shall never hold such a dear place in my heart as Lady Augusta does." He saw the way Miss Trevelyan's hands clenched into fists but felt nothing but a quiet satisfaction building in his heart, knowing now that he had come to the close of the mystery and finding himself more than a little satisfied. "You have both manipulated and controlled those around you to try to gain what you want, but it is not to be. Your plans have failed. You will not succeed. Your struggles have been in vain and now there is nothing left but your shame."

He watched Miss Trevelyan and Lady Villiers exchange a glance, knowing full well what they now thought. The fear on their faces told him that they knew what he now threatened and whilst he had no intention of doing such a thing just to spite them, the warning was clear enough for them to understand.

"What will you do, Lord Leicestershire?"

Lady Villiers' voice was trembling now, one arm wrapped around her daughter's arm as she looked up at him, all boldness gone. Stephen looked down at Lady Augusta and saw the anger held in her eyes. Pressing her hand, he gestured for her to speak her mind, trusting that she would be able to speak with eloquence despite her upset.

"You have tormented Miss Sidwell," Lady Augusta said, gesturing to the young lady who was still being comforted by Lady Mary. "Lord Drake has had a promise from you, Miss Trevelyan, which you have yet to fulfill. Lady Claverhouse has coin to receive, which I am sure you have not yet bestowed upon her." She threw him a quick look and then returned her gaze to Miss Trevelyan. "You will do as you have promised, and you will give Lady Claverhouse what you owe. As for Miss Sidwell..." Looking back at the young lady, Stephen saw that she looked at Lady Augusta with a glimmer of fear in her eyes but smiled at her in reassurance.

"You will leave Miss Sidwell and her family alone," Lady Augusta continued firmly. "She will be my acquaintance and I shall do all I can to help her gain a suitable match so that your power over her will no longer be a threat." She gave Miss Sidwell a small smile, only for the lady to burst into fresh tears, although Stephen suspected it came from relief at Lady Augusta's pronouncement, rather than anything else.

"You have nothing to fear any longer, Miss Sidwell," he told her as she gave Lady Mary a very watery smile. "Lady Villiers, Miss Trevelyan, your remaining within society is now contingent on you doing precisely what Lady Augusta has stated. If you do not, then I shall have no hesitation in revealing to the *ton* all that has occurred, all that you have done." He saw the mother and daughter exchange glances and knew that his threat, whilst sounding less than severe, held a great weight of consequence. Miss Trevelyan would be shunned from society and never able to make a good match, whilst Lady Villiers would be forced to remain in her estate and struggle to make any return to the *beau monde*. The rumors and whispers about them both would last for a good many years until perhaps Miss Trevelyan was close to spinsterhood.

"We..." Lady Villiers looked at her daughter, clearly

resigning herself to agreeing to what Lady Augusta and he had said. "We will do as you ask, Lady Augusta, of course."

Lady Augusta bristled, her eyes narrowed. "Then there is no reason for you to linger here," she stated as the tension in the room rose all the higher, with every eye lingering on Lady Villiers and Miss Trevelyan. "Depart at once and remember what you are expected to do."

"I will make certain that all that has been asked of you has been fulfilled," Stephen reminded them, as Lady Villiers dropped into a curtsy—as though such a gracious action would grant them any sort of forgiveness, as if he might be a little softened by her respective gesture. "Ensure that you see to it at once."

Miss Trevelyan did *not* curtsy, a hint of defiance in her eyes. Her jaw set, she turned on her heel and strode from the bookshop, leaving Lady Villiers to scurry after her daughter. Everyone else watched the door shut behind them, silence filling the bookshop. Stephen let out a long sigh of relief.

"I do not think you need linger either, Lady Whitaker," he said firmly, as the lady's eyes flared for a moment before she dropped her head and made for the door. "And you, Lord Drake..." He let the silence linger for a moment as he looked at the gentleman with anger lurking deep within his heart, recalling what the man had attempted to do to Lady Augusta. Much to his surprise, the gentleman dropped his head and averted his gaze, perhaps a little ashamed of his behavior.

"It may not mean a great deal, Lady Augusta," Lord

Drake said, moving towards her and bowing low, "but I am a little sorry for what I attempted to do."

Lady Augusta blinked in surprise as Stephen rolled his eyes at Lord Drake's ridiculous attempt at an apology.

"I must hope, Lord Drake, that you might consider reforming your ways," she answered, as Lord Drake screwed up his face, a glimmer of mischief back within his eyes. "If there is a lady that you truly consider, then might there be some hope that you can become a true gentleman?"

"One can only hope," Lord Drake replied, inclining his head again before turning towards the door. Without another word, he took his leave, the door shutting heavily behind them all.

"Goodness!" Lady Mary exclaimed, her voice bringing a new light-heartedness to the room and making Stephen smile. "That was all quite extraordinary."

"Indeed it was," Lord Dryden replied with a chuckle, moving towards Lady Mary and Miss Sidwell. "You did very well, Miss Sidwell, I must say."

Lady Augusta nodded and approached the young lady, holding out her hands to her. "I am grateful to you for telling the truth without hesitation," she told her as Miss Sidwell sniffed but held Lady Augusta's gaze. "I cannot imagine how much you have struggled, Miss Sidwell, but I can assure you that it is all at an end now."

Lady Mary pressed Miss Sidwell's arm. "I will return you home now, Miss Sidwell."

"And if it would please you, I will accompany you also," Lord Dryden replied, with Lady Mary's smile warming as she turned to him, accepting his arm without hesitation. Stephen nodded to his friend as he watched them leave together, more certain than ever that his friend would find a true sense of happiness with Lady Mary. He watched the door shut behind them all and turned back towards Lady Augusta, who was moving to him with a warm smile catching the corners of her mouth.

"Lady Augusta," he breathed, coming to take her hands and feeling his heart lift with such a sense of relief that it washed all through him, taking his breath away. He could not speak, finding himself too overcome and looking down into her eyes. Her smile was sparkling, her hands soft in his, and his desire to pull her close to him growing with every moment.

"It appears that it is all at an end, Lord Leicester-shire," Lady Augusta whispered, pressing his hands tightly. "I cannot quite believe it."

"Nor can I," he admitted, feeling as if he were a bird that had been released from a cage and was only now learning what it meant to be free. "I confess that I did not realize it was Miss Trevelyan until last evening when you said something about the perpetrator being a young lady of quality and how she would be acquainted with certain people." With a small shake of his head, he gave a sigh. "But to know that Lady Villiers was also involved was something of a surprise. And I certainly knew nothing about my brother and his arrangement with Miss Trevelyan."

Lady Augusta held his gaze. "And do you think that your brother meant to marry her?"

Stephen shook his head without hesitation. "No, I do

not," he said softly, knowing well that his brother had been a cad. There was no denying that, and the more he thought of it, the more certain he became that his brother had never meant to even encourage Miss Trevelyan. Most likely, he had promised her such a thing as courtship and beyond that, the hope of marriage, in order to extricate himself from her company when she had become too eager. "But that does not mean that Miss Trevelyan had any right to do what she did."

"No, of course not," Lady Augusta replied swiftly. "I am only glad that we have been able to bring her grip on these circumstances to an end—and so that we might help Miss Sidwell also."

Unable to help himself, Stephen pulled his hand gently from hers and then touched her cheek, seeing the flush that came into her face almost at once. "I think very highly of you for your kindness, Lady Augusta," he told her, wanting to express the truths of his heart to her. "You and I have had something of a bumpy path together, but we have managed to come to a place of happiness in the end."

"And to a place of love."

He caught his breath, blinking rapidly and wondering if he had heard her speak those words or if he had imagined it. It was only when she smiled and settled one hand over his heart that he knew he had not been mistaken.

"It may come as something of a surprise to you, Leicestershire, but I confess that I love you," she said without even a hint of embarrassment. "It is not an emotion I ever imagined would fill my heart, but it has come upon me with such steadiness that it is now something I cannot deny. It is within my heart and within my soul. And it is not something that I believe will ever leave me. I look forward to our wedding day because it will be a time when I can make my vows knowing that they are made with love and with a deep joy that fills my heart."

Stephen did not know what to say, finding it hard to respond to such a statement. It was not that he did not feel the same but that he found himself so overcome by it that it robbed him of speech. His breathing was ragged, his chest tight, and his whole body filled with an extraordinary tension.

"I do not say such a thing to have you say it in kind," Lady Augusta said hastily, her eyes suddenly rounding, a look of anxiety coming into her eyes. "It is only because I wished to express my heart to you, Leicestershire, not because I—"

He silenced her with a kiss. His lips met hers, his mouth pressed down with fervor, and felt her melt against him. Her arms went about his neck as he held her tight around the waist, pulling her close. Angling his head, he deepened their kiss, feeling every part of him cry out with a resounding love and affection for the lady he held in his arms. There was nothing more that he wanted save for this, save for Lady Augusta. She was everything to him now, had become all that he needed, all that he desired. Their future together was a joy to consider, their lives shared as one bringing him more happiness than he had ever experienced the more he thought of it. It was a bright light shining ahead of him, a precious gift that was just waiting for him to open. Stephen felt blessed beyond measure that he would get to spend his days with Lady Augusta as his wife, desperate to make certain that he treated her with all the love and kindness that she deserved.

"In case you are unaware of what this means, Lady Augusta," he whispered against her mouth, his eyes still closed, "it is my way of attempting to tell you that my love for you is deep within my heart also." Lifting his head back slowly, he looked at her and saw her eyes open. There was such a look of wonder in her eyes that he could not help but laugh with the sheer joy of it, resting his forehead against hers. "It is true, my love," he said again, wanting her to believe it without hesitation. "I love you most ardently, my dear Augusta. I can hardly wait until the day that we wed so that I can spend every day, every moment with you. I am most eager for you to be my wife so that I might be your husband, so that I might cover you with the love that has arrested my heart."

Lady Augusta let out a long, slow breath that danced across his cheek. Her eyes held the stars, sparkling with all the joyous emotion that had captured her.

"I can hardly believe it," she answered him, lifting one hand to brush down his cheek before returning to the back of his head, her fingers curling through his hair. "We are a love match after all."

"Indeed we are," he told her, smiling gently. "I have never been more grateful for anyone or anything in my life before, Lady Augusta. You have shared your heart with me, and I have found myself eager to love you." Bending his head, he reached down to kiss her again, his heart turning over in his chest as she reached for him, her face lifted for his kiss.

"I love you, Leicestershire," she whispered against his mouth, her eyes closed and her hands holding him tightly. "I love you with all of my heart."

"As I love you," he replied before catching her up in his arms once more.

A SNEAK PEEK OF A NEW BEGINNING

CHAPTER ONE

"Good evening, Miss Taylor."

Miss Emily Taylor, daughter to the Viscount Chesterton, kept her gaze low to the ground, her stomach knotting. The gentleman who had greeted her was, at this present moment, looking at her with something akin to a leer, his balding head already gleaming in the candlelight.

"Good evening, Lord Smithton," she murmured, hearing the grunt from her father than indicated she should be doing more than simply acknowledging the gentleman's presence. The last thing Emily wished to do, however, was to encourage the man any further. He was, to her eyes, grotesque, and certainly not a suitable match for someone who had only recently made her debut, even *if* he was a Marquess.

"Emily is delighted to see you this evening," her father said, giving Emily a small push forward. "I am certain she will be glad to dance with you whenever you wish!"

Emily closed her eyes, resisting the urge to step back

from the fellow, in the knowledge that should she do so, her father would make certain that consequences would follow. She could not bring herself to speak, almost feeling Lord Smithton's eyes roving over her form as she opened her eyes and kept her gaze low.

"You know very well that I would be more than pleased to accompany you to the floor," Lord Smithton said, his voice low and filled with apparent longing. Emily suppressed a shudder, forcing herself to put her hand out and let her dance card drop from her wrist. Lord Smithton, however, did not grasp her dance card but took her hand in his, making a gasp escape from her mouth. The swift intake of breath from behind her informed Emily that she was not alone in her surprise and shock, for her mother also was clearly very upset that Lord Smithton had behaved in such an improper fashion. Her father, however, said nothing and, in the silence that followed, allowed himself a small chuckle.

Emily wanted to weep. It was obvious that her father was not about to say a single word about Lord Smithton's improper behavior. Instead, it seemed he was encouraging it. Her heart ached with the sorrow that came from having a father who cared so little for her that he would allow impropriety in front of so many of the *beau monde*. Her reputation could be stained from such a thing, whispers spread about her, and yet her father would stand by and allow them to go about her without even a twinge of concern.

Most likely, this was because his intention was for Emily to wed Lord Smithton. It had been something Emily had begun to suspect during these last two weeks, for Lord Smithton had been present at the same social gatherings as she had attended with her parents, and her father had always insisted that she greet him. Nothing had been said as yet, however, which came as something of a relief, but deep down, Emily feared that her father would simply announce one day that she was engaged to the old, leering Lord Smithton.

"Wonderful," Lord Smithton murmured, finally letting go of Emily's hand and grasping her dance card. "I see that you have no others as yet, Miss Taylor."

"We have only just arrived," said Emily's mother, from just behind Emily. "That is why –"

"I am certain that Lord Smithton does not need to know such things," Lord Chesterton interrupted, silencing Emily's mother immediately. "He is clearly grateful that Emily has not yet had her head turned by any other gentleman as yet."

Closing her eyes tightly, Emily forced herself to breathe normally, aware of how Lord Smithton chuckled at this. She did not have any feelings of attraction or even fondness for Lord Smithton but yet her father was stating outright that she was interested in Lord Smithton's attentions!

"I have chosen the quadrille, the waltz and the supper dance, Miss Taylor."

Emily's eyes shot open, and she practically jerked back the dance card from Lord Smithton's hands, preventing him from finishing writing his name in the final space. Her father stiffened beside her, her mother gasping in shock, but Emily did not allow either reaction to prevent her from keeping her dance card away from Lord Smithton.

"I am afraid I cannot permit such a thing, Lord Smithton," she told him plainly, her voice shaking as she struggled to find the confidence to speak with the strength she needed. "Three dances would, as you know, send many a tongue wagging and I cannot allow such a thing to happen. I am quite certain you will understand." She lifted her chin, her stomach twisting this way and that in fright as Lord Smithton narrowed his eyes and glared at her.

"My daughter is quite correct, Lord Smithton," Lady Chesterton added, settling a cold hand on Emily's shoulder. "Three dances are, as you know, something that the *ton* will notice and discuss without dissention."

Emily held her breath, seeing how her father and Lord Smithton exchanged a glance. Her eyes began to burn with unshed tears but she did not allow a single one to fall. She was trying to be strong, was she not? Therefore, she could not allow herself to show Lord Smithton even a single sign of weakness.

"I suppose that is to be understood," Lord Smithton said, eventually, forcing a breath of relief to escape from Emily's chest, weakening her. "Given that I have not made my intentions towards you clear, Miss Taylor."

The weakness within her grew all the more. "Intentions?" she repeated, seeing the slow smile spreading across Lord Smithton's face and feeling almost sick with the horror of what was to come.

Lord Smithton took a step closer to her and reached for her hand, which Emily was powerless to refuse. His eyes were fixed on hers, his tongue running across his lower lip for a moment before he spoke.

"Your father and I have been in discussions as regards your dowry and the like, Miss Taylor," he explained, his hand tightening on hers. "We should come to an agreement very soon, I am certain of it."

Emily closed her eyes tightly, feeling her mother's hand still resting on her shoulder and forcing herself to focus on it, to feel the support that she needed to manage this moment and all the emotions that came with it.

"We shall be wed before Season's end," Lord Smithton finished, grandly, as though Emily would be delighted with such news. "We shall be happy and content, shall we not, Miss Taylor?"

The lump in Emily's throat prevented her from saying anything. She wanted to tell Lord Smithton that he had not even asked her to wed him, had not considered her answer, but the words would not come to her lips. Of course, she would have no choice in the matter. Her father would make certain of that.

"You are speechless, of course," Lord Smithton chuckled, as her father grunted his approval. "I know that this will come as something of a surprise that I have denied myself towards marrying someone such as you, but I have no doubt that we shall get along rather famously." His chuckle became dark, his hand tightening on hers until it became almost painful. "You are an obedient sort, are you not?"

"She is," Emily heard her father say, as she opened her eyes to see Lord Smithton's gaze running over her form. She had little doubt as to what he was referring to, for her mother had already spoken to her about what a husband would require from his wife, and the very thought terrified her.

"Take her, now."

Lord Smithton let go of Emily's hand and gestured towards Lady Chesterton, as though she were his to order about.

"Take her to seek some refreshment. She looks somewhat pale." He laughed and then turned away to speak to Emily's father again, leaving Emily and her mother standing together.

Emily's breathing was becoming ragged, her heart trembling within her as she struggled to fight against the dark clouds that were filling her heart and mind. To be married to such an odious gentleman as Lord Smithton was utterly terrifying. She would have no joy in her life any longer, not even an ounce of happiness in her daily living. Was this her doing? Was it because she had not been strong enough to stand up to her own father and refuse to do as he asked? Her hands clenched hard, her eyes closing tightly as she fought to contain the sheer agony that was deep within her heart.

"My dear girl, I am so dreadfully sorry."

Lady Chesterton touched her arm but Emily jerked away, her eyes opening. "I cannot marry Lord Smithton, Mama."

"You have no choice," Lady Chesterton replied, sadly, her own eyes glistening. "I have tried to speak to your father but you know the sort of gentleman he is."

"Then I shall run away," Emily stated, fighting against the desperation that filled her. "I cannot remain."

Lady Chesterton said nothing for a moment or two, allowing Emily to realize the stupidity of what she had said. There was no-one else to whom she could turn to, no-one else to whom she might escape. The only choices that were open to her were either to do as her father asked or to find another who might marry her instead – and the latter gave her very little hope.

Unless Lord Havisham....

The thought was pushed out of her mind before she could begin to consider it. She had become acquainted with Lord Havisham over the few weeks she had been in London and he had appeared very attentive. He always sought her out to seek a dance or two, found her conversation engaging and had even called upon her on more than one occasion. But to ask him to consider marrying her was something that Emily simply could not contemplate. He would think her rude, foolish and entirely improper, particularly when she could not be certain that he had any true affection for her.

But if you do nothing, then Lord Smithton will have his way.

"Emily."

Her mother's voice pulled her back to where she stood, seeing the pity and the helplessness in her mother's eyes and finding herself filling with despair as she considered her future.

"I do not want to marry Lord Smithton," Emily said again, tremulously. "He is improper, rude and I find myself afraid of him." She saw her mother drop her head, clearly struggling to find any words to encourage Emily. "What am I to do, mama?"

"I – I do not know." Lady Chesterton looked up slowly, a single tear running down her cheek. "I would save you from this if I could, Emily but there is nothing I can do or say that will prevent your father from forcing this upon you."

Emily felt as though a vast, dark chasm had opened up underneath her feet, pulling her down into it until she could barely breathe. The shadows seemed to fill her lungs, reaching in to tug at her heart until it beat so quickly that she felt as though she might faint.

"I must go," Emily whispered, reaching out to grasp her mother's hand for a moment. "I need a few minutes alone." She did not wait for her mother to say anything, to give her consent or refusal, but hurried away without so much as a backward look. She walked blindly through the crowd of guests, not looking to the left or to the right but rather straight ahead, fixing her gaze on her goal. The open doors that led to the dark gardens.

The cool night air brushed at her hot cheeks but Emily barely noticed. Wrapping her arms about her waist, she hurried down the steps and then sped across the grass, not staying on the paths that wound through the gardens themselves. She did not know where she was going, only that she needed to find a small, dark, quiet space where she might allow herself to think and to cry without being seen.

She soon found it. A small arbor kept her enclosed as she sank down onto the small wooden bench. No sound other than that of strains of music and laughter from the ballroom reached her ears. Leaning forward, Emily felt herself begin to crumble from within, her heart aching and her mind filled with despair. There was no way out. There was nothing she could do. She would have to marry Lord Smithton and, in doing so, would bring herself more sadness and pain than she had ever felt before.

There was no-one to rescue her. There was no-one to save her. She was completely and utterly alone.

CHAPTER TWO

Three days later and Emily had stopped her weeping and was now staring at herself in the mirror, taking in the paleness of her cheeks and the dullness of her eyes.

Her father had only just now informed her that she was to be wed by the Season's end and was now to consider herself engaged. There had been no discussion. There had been not even a thought as to what she herself might feel as regarded Lord Smithton. It had simply been a matter of course. She was to do as her father had directed, as she had been taught to do.

Emily swallowed hard, closing her eyes tightly as another wave of tears crashed against her closed lids. Was this to be her end? Married to Lord Smithton, a gentleman whom she despised, and allowing herself to be treated in any way he chose? It would be a continuation of her life as it was now. No consideration, no thought was given to her. Expected to do as she was instructed without question – and no doubt the consequences would be severe for her if she did not do as Lord Smithton expected.

A shudder ran through her and Emily opened her eyes. For the first time, a small flickering flame of anger ignited and began to burn within her. Was she simply going to allow this to be her life? Was she merely going to step aside and allow Lord Smithton and her father to come to this arrangement without her acceptance? Was she truly as weak as all that?

Heat climbed up her spine and into her face. Weak was a word to describe her, yes. She *was* weak. She had tried, upon occasion, to do as she pleased instead of what her father had demanded of her and the punishment each time had broken her spirit all the more until she had not even a single thought about disobeying him. It had been what had led to this circumstance. If she had been stronger, if she had been more willing to accept the consequences of refusing to obey her father without question without allowing such a thing to break her spirit, then would she be as she was now?

"Then mayhap there is a time yet to change my circumstances."

The voice that came from her was weak and tremulous but with a lift of her chin, Emily told herself that she needed to try and find some courage if she was to find any hope of escaping Lord Smithton. And the only thought she had was that of Lord Havisham.

Viscount Havisham was, of course, lower in title and wealth than the Marquess of Smithton, but that did not matter to Emily. They had discovered a growing acquaintance between them, even though it was not often that her father had let her alone to dance and converse with another gentleman. It had been a blessing that the requests to call upon her had come at a time when her father had been resting from the events of the previous evening, for her and her mother had been able to arrange for him to call when Lord Chesterton had been gone from the house. However, nothing of consequence had ever been shared between them and he certainly had not, as yet, made his request to court her but mayhap it had simply been too soon for such a decision. Regardless, Emily could not pretend that they did not enjoy a comfortable acquaintance, with easy conversation and many warm glances shared between them. In truth, her heart fluttered whenever she laid eyes upon him, for his handsome features and his broad smile had a profound effect upon her.

It was her only chance to escape from Lord Smithton. She had to speak to Lord Havisham and lay her heart bare. She had to trust that he too had a fondness for her, in the same way that she had found her affections touched by him. Else what else was she to do?

Lifting her chin, Emily closed her eyes and took in a long breath to steady herself. After a moment of quiet reflection, she rose and made her way to the writing table in the corner of the bedchamber, sitting down carefully and picking up her quill.

"Miss Taylor."

Emily's breath caught as she looked up into Lord

Havisham's face. His dark blue eyes held a hint of concern, his smile somewhat tensed as he bowed in greeting.

"Lord Havisham," she breathed, finding even his very presence to be overwhelming. "You received my note, then."

"I did," he replied, with a quick smile, although a frown began to furrow his brow. "You said that it was of the utmost importance that we spoke this evening."

Emily nodded, looking about her and seeing that her father was making his way up the small staircase towards the card room, walking alongside Lord Smithton. Their engagement was to be announced later this evening and Emily knew she had to speak to Lord Havisham before that occurred.

"I know this is most untoward, but might we speak in private?" she asked, reaching out and surreptitiously putting her hand on his arm, battling against the fear of impropriety. She had done this much, she told herself. Therefore, all she had to do was continue on as she had begun and her courage might be rewarded.

Lord Havisham hesitated. "That may be a little...."

Emily blushed furiously, knowing that to speak alone with a gentleman was not at all correct, for it could bring damaging consequences to them both – but for her, at this moment, she did not find it to be a particularly concerning issue, given that she was to be married to Lord Smithton if he did not do anything.

"It is of the greatest importance, as I have said," she replied, quickly, praying that he would consent. "Please, Lord Havisham, it will not take up more than a few minutes of your time." Seeing him hesitate even more, she bit her lip. "Surely you must know me well enough to know that I would not force you into anything, Lord Havisham," she pleaded, noting how his eyes darted away from hers, a slight flush now in his cheeks. "There is enough of a friendship between us, is there not?"

Lord Havisham nodded and then sighed "I am sorry, Miss Taylor," he replied, quietly, looking at her. "You are quite right. Come. The gardens will be quiet."

Walking away from her mother – who did not do anything to hinder Emily's departure, Emily felt such an overwhelming sense of relief that it was all she could do to keep her composure. Surely Lord Havisham, with his goodness and kind nature, would see the struggle that faced her and seek to do what he could to bring her aid? Surely he had something of an affection in his heart for her? But would it be enough?

"Now," Lord Havisham began, as they stepped outside. "What is it that troubles you so, Miss Taylor?"

Now that it came to it, Emily found her mouth going dry and her heart pounding so furiously that she could barely speak. She looked up at Lord Havisham, seeing his features only slightly in the darkness of the evening and found herself desperately trying to say even a single word.

"It is....." Closing her eyes, she halted and dragged in air, knowing that she was making a complete cake of herself.

"I am to be wed to Lord Smithton," she managed to say, her words tumbling over each other in an attempt to be spoken. "I have no wish to marry him but my father insists upon it." Opening her eyes, she glanced warily up at Lord Havisham and saw his expression freeze.

Find out what happens next between Emily and Lord Havisham in the book, available in the Kindle Store A New Beginning

JOIN MY MAILING LIST

Sign up for my newsletter to stay up to date on new releases, contests, giveaways, freebies, and deals!

Free book with signup!

Monthly Facebook Giveaways! Books and Amazon gift cards!
Join me on Facebook: https://www. facebook.com/rosepearsonauthor

Website: www.RosePearsonAuthor.com

Follow me on Goodreads: Author Page

You can also follow me on Bookbub!
Click on the picture below – see the Follow button?